Bittersweet CONFESSIONS

CHESSA ANDERSEN

FOR HEATHER TURVEY
FOR INTRODUCING ME TO THE
BEAUTIFUL AND DELICIOUS WORLD
OF BLENDED COFFEE DRINKS.

FOR BHAKTI DEOTALE.
YOU ARE STRONG.
YOU ARE BEAUTIFUL.
YOU ARE ENOUGH.

But First, Coffee

"You are strong. You are beautiful," I said dreamily, sitting alone at a round table on the spacious patio outside of the cafeteria at work.

My lunch hour was my favorite part of the day. I enjoyed the solitude when the hectic lunch crowd thinned out. I wasn't a brooding loner or anything; I occasionally had lunch with a few people from work. A book and a cup of coffee was all I needed to recharge myself for the rest of the day.

"Buck up, buttercup," a familiar voice said brightly, interrupting my relaxing chant.

Summer Bradlee set a tall clear plastic cup filled with delicious-looking caramel cold brew in front of me, and my heart raced at the sight of pure beauty.

Hello, gorgeous, I thought to myself with a big smile.

"There's the smile I adore and love," Summer declared, grinning and throwing her tiny little body into a chair next to mine.

"Thank you, Summer."

Her name accurately described my co-worker – a bright ray of warm sunshine packaged in a five-foot five cute brunette with wide chocolate brown eyes and dimples whenever she flashed a genuine smile.

"You are strong," she said seriously. "You are beautiful, Cat. Don't forget that."

"Uh, I was talking about my coffee," I admitted, looking down at my almost-finished fourth cup of coffee in my hands.

Summer laughed, and I swallowed the last of the lukewarm beverage to enjoy the fresh cold brew.

"Of course, you were," she said, sipping her own caramel cold brew. "Listen, Cat, hang in there. I know this wasn't what you expected when you were hired full time."

What I expected when I accepted the paid position was becoming a full-fledged interior designer with a wise and kind mentor and amazingly creative projects. Instead my duties remained exactly the same when I was an unpaid intern last year: sorting and delivering mail and making numerous coffee runs. Except now I had my own computer and desk.

I spent last year working my ass off at Ward Designs, a highly reputable interior design business, and studying to graduate with honors at the local university. I honestly believed my time and effort would be rewarded with something good. I was an idiot.

I reluctantly accepted my fate last week when the boss' fourth personal assistant in a year ran out of the office in tears. According to Summer, the boss specifically demanded "that coffee girl" become her temporary personal assistant until a new team of interns was chosen.

"You really are a great asset to the team," Summer reassured me. "Everyone likes you, and you've been doing a great job."

It's not that hard to sort and deliver mail, I thought sourly. *Plus, I actually don't mind making the coffee runs as I am a self-diagnosed coffee addict.*

"Plus, you were the only intern that had been hired full time," she pointed out proudly, making me feel slightly ashamed of my rotten attitude.

"Thanks," I said, feeling a tiny bit better, as I thought about the other four interns that didn't know what to do after graduation.

The others had been envious and surprised about the job offer, but I knew that would disappear quickly once they heard my duties stayed the same. I wouldn't be surprised if they placed bets on how long I would last now that I was at the boss' beck and call.

"Anytime, kiddo," she said, standing up and adjusting her pale pink skirt that complemented the dark pink blouse. "I need you to be completely honest with me, Cat."

I swallowed hard and matched her intense gaze, not knowing what truth Summer wanted. Was my job making me miserable and slowly killing my dream one day at a time? Yes. A million times yes. Should I be honest about my feelings? My instincts screamed no. A million times no.

"Do I look like cotton candy?" Summer asked, waving her hands over her outfit in one dramatic sweep. "Is this too much pink? I feel like it's too much pink."

I grinned and shook my head. "No, Summer. You look perfect as always."

"Are you sure? You're not just saying that because I sign your paychecks?"

"I have direct deposit."

"Who approves your direct deposit?" she countered teasingly, placing her hands on her hips.

"Point taken," I admitted in defeat. "Seriously, you look great to the point that I really want to hate you."

"Really?" she asked, with mock excitement and a wide smile. "I wish we could be archenemies, but I like you too much."

I laughed, shaking my head again. Summer looked beyond the patio, breathing in the fresh air.

"What a beautiful day. The office is kinda slow so take your time. okay?"

"Thanks, Summer. I'll see you upstairs."

I could barely contain my giddiness of spending extra time with my book and cold brew.

"Hello, handsome," she purred behind me as I heard the glass door from the cafeteria to the patio open and close.

I shook my head and smiled at Summer's harmless nickname for any hot guy that crossed her path.

"Catherine Coleman?" a deep unfamiliar voice asked uncertainly.

I refrained from scrunching my nose and sighing deeply at the second interruption as I tilted my head to stare at a tall and extremely attractive man with dark blonde hair and piercing green eyes. My mind raced around frantically, believing the clean cut face wearing an amused grin looked a little familiar. And my heart decided to slow down dramatically, thinking this was the right time to die.

"Uh, yes," I squeaked out like a junior high tween. "Cat."

"I remember you from high school," the familiar stranger said casually, lowering himself in Summer's now vacant chair, with a covered paper coffee cup in his hands. "You graduated with my sister. Gail Greenlaw."

Ugh. Gail Greenlaw. I thought bitterly, unable to stop my brown eyes from rolling. *This day truly sucks ... wait, what? Sister?*

"David?" I asked incredulously, studying his handsome features again and remembering a scrawny kid with chicken legs.

Even though David Greenlaw was two years younger than me, I remembered him from my years on the high school cross country team. I had been a freshman when he joined as a seventh grader. He had been a tiny kid with unruly blonde hair and a baby face, but he had heart and determination when it came to running.

And now he looked absolutely nothing like that kid. Wearing the absolute hell out of a light gray business suit with a white button down shirt and skinny black tie, David exuded confidence and poise with over six-foot height and hard body most likely chiseled from granite.

Little David Greenlaw was now very much a sexy, sexy man.

"Holy shit, David!" I exclaimed with surprise, leaning back in my chair and smiling uncontrollably. "What are you doing here?"

He and I were a good seven- or eight-hour drive away from our hometown in northern Minnesota.

"School and then work," he explained, absentmindedly rotating the coffee cup in his large hands. "Well, technically, not work. I just started an internship at Armstead Architecture while I finish school."

"Wow. That's impressive. I'm surprised the firm hasn't taken over another floor of the building."

Really, Cat? That's the best response you could come up with? I silently admonished myself. *Ask questions about him not the stupid office building.*

The wealthy and talented genius behind Armstead Architecture also designed and built the highly sophisticated eight-story office building that housed his architecture firm on the top floor and other businesses on the floors below.

"What about you?" David asked. "Do you work on one of the floors?"

"I work on the fifth floor. Ward Designs."

"You used to draw, didn't you? I remember you always sketching something on the bus to cross country meets."

"Yeah," I admitted, wondering if I should be impressed or worried he had a memory of me. "I still like to sketch. I'm working my way up from lowly intern to fabulous interior designer."

"Hey, we all have to start somewhere, right?"

I nodded in agreement, enjoying his laid-back and casual demeanor.

"I'm glad I noticed you out here," David said, taking a sip from his coffee cup. "It's nice to see a familiar face in a new area."

"How long have you been in Iowa?"

He squeezed one of his beautiful green eyes shut for a nanosecond as he thought about the question. "It will be one year in September. After high school, I spent two years at the technical college and found myself fascinated with architecture. My advisor recommended the program at the university down here."

"Kind of a long way from home," I hedged, hoping he would drop a tiny hint about his evil sister's whereabouts.

I desperately wished she was anywhere else in the world or she considered Iowa was too far beneath her that she wouldn't dare step across the state border. One could only dream.

David shrugged slightly. "I'm okay with that."

His tone suggested he had a few more reasons for moving, but I didn't press the subject. I had my own reasons for purposely distancing myself from our hometown too. I wanted to be anywhere but there; I just didn't believe I would live in Iowa of all states.

"A few other students and I were chosen for the summer internship," he shared, slowly tapping his long fingers on the table. "So I'll be around here until school starts in the fall."

"Cool," I said, nodding slightly. "I'm always here."

"Maybe we can hang out sometime?"

A million times yes! Yes! Yes! My heart sang with happiness.

Knock it off, my calm and collected mind warned. *Devastatingly handsome men literally swarm the building every day.*

The thought of actually engaging in a conversation with a devastatingly handsome man made my palms sweaty and my stomach flutter with a mix of excitement and nervousness. The words "excuse me" automatically tumbled out of my mouth whenever I crossed paths with any gorgeous guy in an expensive suit. Talking wasn't the problem. Holding a personal conversation was a completely different story.

I wasn't a complete dummy. I knew my exotic looks and somewhat shapely ass caught many men's attention. My dad gifted me with his Korean genes: thick dark hair, warm brown eyes, and natural slender frame.

My mom who was born and raised in Minnesota gave me her Midwestern genes: pale complexion that burned easily in the sun, above average height (almost six feet tall in high heels), and full pouty lips.

Thanks to different groups of professionals that love to gossip over lunch, I knew the majority of the business men were cocky narcissistic assholes that didn't think twice about cheating on a girlfriend or wife. Because of the stories and the numerous times I caught someone in a suit staring at my ass and boobs, I shied away from any man working in the building.

After glancing at my watch, I stood up and collected my book and cold brew. "Sorry. My lunch break is over. I gotta get back to work."

"No problem, Cat," David said, giving me a wide smile, as I noticed his eyes quickly drifting over my figure. "Do you always take your lunch break this late?"

I nodded, mentally grateful for the professional dress code. I wore a high-waisted white skirt with a faint black plaid design and a simple black wrapped shirt with white high heels. Something simple and comfortable but yet professional.

Normally I would be irritated when men openly gape at me as if I was a stripper throwing herself around a pole. But I decided to give David a break since he probably hadn't seen me since high school. At least he was trying to be subtle.

"Cool," he said. "I'll see you around I guess."

"It was nice running into you," I said lamely before heading inside the air-conditioned cafeteria.

Keep it together, Catherine Cynthia Coleman, I silently warned myself. *Don't look back at him. Whatever you do, don't …*

My head completely ignored the little warning in my brain and looked over my shoulder in David's direction. He was leaning back in the chair with his long probably non-chicken legs stretched out, and he was looking at me! He smiled and gave me a short wave. I waved shyly before hurrying out of the cafeteria.

I am such a moron! Moron! I admonished myself, stepping into the public elevator and punching the button for the fifth floor.

Sinking my teeth into my lower lip to keep myself from grinning like an idiot, I realized my day just became a little bit better.

"Spill it, Cat," Summer commanded, plopping her tiny tush on my well-organized desk. "Tell me everything! Everything!"

I quickly finished reading an email addressed to my boss before focusing on Summer and her endless enthusiasm for office gossip.

During my orientation as an intern last year, I learned Summer served as the accountant for Ward Designs, handing out company credit cards, gathering various receipts, and figuring out numbers and statistics. But officially, she was Paige Ward's best friend; the one – and only – person in the company who could talk back to the boss without any repercussions.

A few months later after adjusting to basically running errands for the designers and learning absolutely nothing about interior design, the other interns and I gave up hope of impressing anyone with our open and eager minds. While the others routinely arrived to work on time and left promptly at five each day, I stayed late to complete the grunt work that technically could've waited until the next day.

One night Summer literally dragged me out of the office and took me to dinner, where she talked freely about her friendship with the boss. Friends since college, they had seen each other through divorces, breakups, and other failures. When Summer struggled through her second divorce, Paige convinced her to move to Iowa with a lucrative job offer.

Summer knew her best friend intimidated the hell out of her staff and understood they would be wary of her, knowing whatever they said about work would go straight to the boss. But the short cute brunette with her easygoing nature and gift for gab knocked down their walls and, oddly enough, became everyone's confidant.

"What are you talking about?" I asked, scanning the boss' office for her holy presence, but remembered she was in the conference room with some of the designers. "I don't know anything. I get all my gossip from you."

"The hottie at lunch," Summer said, her eyes wide with curiosity. "He's way too young for me, but I suppose I could have some fun with him."

I laughed, leaning back in my chair and relaxing for a moment. Vowing to never get married again, Summer preferred no-strings-attached re-lationships and promptly ended it when the guy wanted something real.

"I saw him sit at your table," she said slyly, genuinely interested. "So, tell me everything."

I shrugged nonchalantly. "There's really nothing to tell. Just someone from my hometown."

"Wisconsin?"

"Minnesota," I corrected, knowing Summer wouldn't remember the tidbit anyway.

"Are you going to see him again?" she asked after I basically repeated my conversation with David to her.

"Probably around the building."

Summer dramatically rolled her eyes and pushed my black leather rolling chair back with her foot. "Outside of work, you dummy."

"Oh, I dunno," I admitted, scooting my chair back toward the desk. "I haven't had a chance to think about it."

"What's there to think about? You're both young and dumb."

"Hey!"

"Not intellectually dumb," she clarified, glancing at my non-personalized desk. "Dumb as in you're both young and should do dumb stuff."

"That daily self-help calendar really comes in handy, doesn't it," I teased.

"Why wouldn't you want to see what happens next?"

Gail. His sister. Ugh.

I frowned, remembering all the times Gail embarrassed me or made me feel small in high school. We weren't bitter rivals or anything. We ran in different social circles; she was obviously the queen bee in the popular clique. My friends and I fell somewhere in the middle; we weren't really nerds, rebels, or popular. We were just – normal.

The school was big enough that we rarely had classes together, but it was small enough to know most of the classmates. If Gail had a serious problem with me like the way she did with Angelique Ferris our freshman year, she would've let me and the entire school know about it.

Believing she was auditioning for the dance team, Angelique erotically writhed and seductively strutted across the stage – a routine she insisted the captain taught her – during the talent show also being held that day. About two minutes into her performance, she realized the entire student body was watching her prance around in thigh-high latex boots, booty shorts, and a crop top. She ran off the stage in tears.

As the principal reprimanded her – and eventually suspended her for a week – for the inappropriate peepshow, Angelique tried in vain to blame Gail. After pulling herself together in the bathroom, Angelique and two of her friends ran into the queen bee who allegedly said, "That's what you get for fucking my sloppy seconds."

Why did Gail even care about Angelique dating her ex-boyfriend a week after she cruelly dumped him to go out with a senior basketball player anyway? No one but Gail and God knew the answer. That was how the little blonde psychopath operated – without reason.

To this day, I honestly had no idea why I had landed on her bitch radar.

"Where's the queen bee now?" Summer asked, picking up the red stapler on my desk.

"No idea," I said, opening a drawer and rummaging around for a box of staples. "I took off as soon as I graduated. And I make sure my holiday hometown visits are short as possible."

I knew Summer wanted to know more about my strained relationship with my family, but she never pushed me for more details. She could badger anyone into spilling their life story for her, but for some reason, she gave me space. And I respected her for that.

She and I first bonded over our dislike for Iowa – a state filled with corn fields and dedicated Hawkeye fans. To be clear, we had no issues with the people (except asshat drivers), places, cities, or even the scenery. We just didn't like the state.

And, yes, many people had pointed out Minnesota was very similar, but at least the state had three professional sports teams – football, baseball, and basketball – and the Mall of America. Maybe four teams, but I knew very little about hockey.

Summer had even more reasons to dislike Iowa because Paige pulled her away from North Carolina. Just as Summer followed her second husband to the beautiful coastal state that I desperately wanted to visit, I highly suspected Paige moved to Iowa for her first husband. Otherwise what would possess two highly intelligent women who grew up in well populated cities in Tennessee to settle down in Iowa?

"Do you think David has a close relationship with her?" Summer asked, opening her hand for staple refills.

"I hope not," I said quickly – maybe too quickly – trying to remember what David had been like during cross country season. "I really don't know that much about him other that he turned into a strong runner and was a good kid."

"Why didn't she like you? I can't imagine anyone being mean to you."

I raised an eyebrow, questioning her last thought. *Um, how well do you know your best friend?*

"Paige doesn't count," Summer muttered, fiddling with the stapler.

"I have no idea," I admitted. "She didn't really bully me; she just made me feel worthless."

"Like how?"

"Somehow my senior yearbook landed in her greedy little hands and she wrote 'get fucked' in big letters."

I didn't regret tossing the yearbook in the trash after reading her words. By then I had been more than ready to leave everything behind me.

"What a fucking whore," Summer declared, placing my fully stocked stapler back in its place on my desk.

I smiled, appreciating her verbal support.

She hopped off the desk, running her hands through her highlighted brown hair. "Cat – "

"You don't look like cotton candy," I interrupted, rolling my eyes and focusing on some new emails.

"Paige picked this outfit for me," Summer explained, straightening out the knee-length pencil skirt. "We went shopping over the weekend, and I made her buy something that wasn't black or gray. A little color never hurt anyone."

My closet looked like a rainbow exploded all over it. My confidence soared to new heights anytime I wore something bright and fun. Bright colors and pretty dresses were just two of many, many weaknesses.

The conference door opened, and Paige Ward, the fearless and demanding owner of Ward Designs, walked out with confidence and purpose to her glass office.

I needed to badger Summer about their routine beauty care because for two women in their early forties they looked damn young without any medical enhancements. I had researched Paige and her company during the application process for the internship so I knew everything about her even her age. She didn't give a shit about the inconsequential numbers and even cared less about who knew.

My boss used her five-foot ten-inch height to her advantage, never afraid to glare or stare down a man. Her naturally blonde hair was perfectly styled into a sleek, layered long bob. Her dark blue eyes never seemed to show compassion or kindness; they held an unreadable coldness.

"Tall. One shot," Paige barked, without even looking in my direction, before entering her office.

"Same please," Summer said, following her best friend and closing the door.

I grabbed my black slim wristlet that contained the bare essentials for coffee and lunch runs – my phone, building ID badge, and the company credit card – and headed toward the elevator.

Coffee runs gave me a chance to stretch my legs and escape my desk for a few minutes. One of my favorite perks was delicious specialty coffee on the company dime. Whenever the boss wanted coffee, I had approval to grab something for myself.

A thirty-something couple that loved coffee a teeny bit more than me owned and operated Latte Love, a local café located near the building's entrance. Incredibly devoted to good customer service, one section specifically catered to the coffee drinkers on a run with a specialized selection. The other section focused on customers enjoying the morning and needing a light meal. It offered a minimal breakfast and lunch menu and small dining area.

I smiled slightly, watching David enter the express café and stand beside me in line. My heart fluttered a bit at the sight of him with the sleeves of his shirt rolled up and the tie slightly loosened.

"So we meet again," he teased in a sinister and dangerous tone.

"Coffee run?" I asked obviously for lack of a better response.

What the hell is wrong with you? My mind screamed at me.

David ducked his head a little and smiled sheepishly. "I kinda thought an internship meant following architects around and carrying blueprints from one job site to the next."

"Oh, my little grasshopper," I said, with a dramatic sigh. "So young. So much to learn."

"I was organizing some shit when the boss handed me a fifty and said to get some coffee. Fifty is kinda a lot for one cup, right?"

"Oh, grasshopper," I repeated, with a more serious tone, and felt my stomach churn a little. "Do you even know how Mr. Armstead likes his coffee?"

The blank expression on David's face gave me the answer I suspected.

"Is this your first coffee run?" I asked incredulously, wondering if the architectural firm used the "sink or swim" training method.

"The guy who usually did the coffee runs, his internship ended last week, and our paths never crossed," he explained, shrugging casually. "How hard is it to order coffee and give it to the boss?"

"As stupid as this may sound, your boss doesn't have time to mix his own damn coffee. He expects you to know what he likes."

"So, if I give him coffee and some creamer and sugar packets I'll look like an idiot?" David asked in disbelief.

I gave him a sympathetic look, taking a step forward when the line slightly moved.

"All the businesses in the building not only cater to the wealthy and elite, but they're also the best in their respective industry," I said. "The offices were designed to impress the privileged. When you toured the office, did you see a break room? A refrigerator? Or even an area to make coffee?"

David shook his head.

"Most of the businesses don't have a break room because no one wants to keep it clean or even deal with coffee supplies. Also, a break room kind of indicates laziness and inferiority."

"Seriously?"

"Unfortunately, yeah, because a rich client wants to see an office looking busy all the time," I said, with a resigned sigh. "They want to be impressed. Mr. Armstead wasn't a dummy when he designed the building, dedicating an entire floor for the super fancy restaurant."

"But isn't it kinda illegal or something to not have a break room?"

"The cafeteria and the café serve as a collective break room for all the companies. There's even a fancy industrial refrigerator in the cafeteria for people who bring their lunch to work."

"So, what should I do now?"

Even without glancing at the panic in his eyes, I knew I would help him. Taking a deep breath and closing my eyes for a moment, I thought about all the times Christopher Armstead confidently strode into Paige's office. His occasional presence wasn't unusual because they had collaborated on dozen of projects over the past year. I just needed to remember how he liked his coffee.

"David, I really need you to think about the vibe of the office today. Is he in a good mood? Has he yelled at anyone?"

He chewed on his lower lip as he thought about the questions. "I heard him laughing with some guys and talking about the baseball game," he offered.

"That's good." I released a deep breath. "Where did he go after he gave you the money? Did he go to a conference room? His office? Did anyone follow him into his office?"

"I think he went back to his office. By himself."

"You're killing me, grasshopper."

"Hey, Cat," a pretty blonde barista greeted cheerfully. "What do you need now?"

"Hey, Kacey," I said brightly. "I need three tall New England roast with one shot in each please. On a separate check, the guy behind me needs four of the same drink."

"Uh, I just need – " David started to interrupt, but I held up a hand to stop him.

"I love it when you make my job easy," Kacey said, with a wink, as her fingers quickly flew over a tablet screen before bouncing off to fill the orders.

"Thanks, Kace," I called after her before explaining my strong hunch to David. "Take four coffees just in case. When he sees your order, he won't let the good coffee go to waste. He'll probably have you hand it out to certain staff. And if he does have a meeting in his office, your order shows you knew his schedule and were prepared."

"How do you know all this?"

"I learned a thing or two after making coffee runs for over a year," I said, scanning my order on a small tablet screen attached to the counter before sliding the company card through the reader. "If you end up being the intern doing the coffee run, learn his schedule and how he likes his coffee."

"Yes, master," he teased, with a grin.

My mind immediately dove into the gutter, wondering what it would be like to slowly strip off the layers of his clothes and run my hands down his muscled chest faintly seen through the white material of his shirt.

Shit! Was I a pedophile for even fantasizing about doing naughty and possibly dirty things to little David Greenlaw?

Except he wasn't so little anymore as he peered down at me with his beautiful lips forming an all-knowing smirk.

Averting my eyes to keep them from wandering down to a certain body part, I mumbled, "Remember to get a receipt and tip generously."

"Hey, give me your phone."

I frowned slightly but unlocked my phone and placed it in his open hand. Hands I imagined cupping my ass or even spanking me.

Good gracious, I really needed to get laid.

"I'm calling my cell so you have my number."

"Cool," I said, shifting a bit to extinguish the growing heat between my legs. "Let me know how your first coffee run turned out."

As soon as Kacey placed my order on the counter, I made my deliveries and returned to my desk to read through a new set of messages. About an hour later, my phone softly vibrated with a new text message.

David: You saved my ass today.

David: Boss was talking to two guys in his office. Told me to take the last cup.

David: He said nice job, kid.

I smiled, pleased my hunch paid off and David made a good impression.

Cat: Yay! Good job, grasshopper.
David: I owe you.

Happiness hummed through me as I grabbed a huge stack of papers needing to be scanned. Today was definitely a good day.

Stay Grounded

If you stop eating crab rangoons and egg rolls then you don't need to run, the sensible part of my mind lectured sternly.

But Chinese food makes us so happy, the more laid-back part of my brain pointed out.

My normal weekend routine included jogging around my favorite park because of the paved path around a large lake. I loved being near water, and one day, after buying a house, a boat was next on my list. With a steady income established, I looked forward to my unknown future anytime I checked my bank account.

I didn't want to admit it to myself or anyone else for that matter, but I enjoyed catching up with David over lunch and running into him during my coffee runs over the past few weeks. Our easy conversations and flirty and friendly texts definitely made my days fly by quicker and, maybe, a little more fun.

Whenever he stood a smidgen closer or when his hand accidentally brushed mine, I suspected he wanted to ask me out like meet for drinks after work or something. But whatever ran through his head simply bulldozed over my thought like a freight train with a bomb on it. He was no longer next to me, taking a subtle step back or driving his hands into the pocket of his pants.

Or I simply read too much into the awkward moments because my dirty little mind happily skipped ahead a few beats and pushed his head between my legs.

My body had been aching for any kind of attention ever since a gorgeous bartender named Theo ravaged it a few months ago. I wouldn't have minded pursuing something more with him, but he decided to give his cheating ex-girlfriend another chance a week after our little tryst.

My phone softly buzzed in my arm band, and I ignored the text alert and silently yelled at my tired legs to keep moving. But when a steady vibration slightly tickled my sweaty arm, I stopped running and looked at the screen to see an incoming call from David.

"Hello?" I asked breathlessly, stepping off the path to avoid crashing into other runners and pedestrians.

"Cat!" he yelled frantically. "I'm in serious trouble. I didn't know who else to call. Help me!"

"David, calm down. What's going on?" I managed to ask between gasps, using the back of my wrist to wipe a disgustingly amount of sweat from my forehead.

Between him complaining about someone and rambling about a Monday meeting, I pieced together he was at the office trying to create presentation packets.

"This copier is being a huge bitch!" he shouted as I imagined him pacing around the copy room and kicking boxes full of paper. "I made one packet, and then she decided to quit."

"Hey," I snapped, with a smirk he couldn't see. "That's my best friend. She is not a bitch; she's just misunderstood."

Even though the mailroom assistants handled special copy jobs during the week, I had asked them to show me how to use everything in case of emergency. My instincts and curiosity saved my and the other interns' asses whenever we had to work over the weekend and the mailroom staff didn't.

"Cat, please help me. There's no one in the copy room."

Crap, I thought, looking at my outfit of green camo yoga pants and matching dark green sports bra with a gray long-sleeve shirt tied around my waist. I look and probably smell like shit.

If I ran home, showered, and changed, I could be at the office in thirty – maybe forty-five – minutes, but I also knew the park was a good ten minutes away from the office. I frowned at my dilemma, wondering why I wanted to look pretty for David.

"I'll be there in ten minutes," I said reluctantly, starting my run and hoping I wouldn't regret my decision.

"Thank you, Cat!" he sang out gleefully.

"A tall blended caramel frappe with extra whipped cream better be waiting for me."

Before entering the building, I made my ponytail look less messy and pulled on my gray t-shirt. My running attire – purchased on clearance for a mere $20 – wasn't meant to look sexy. The sports bra kept my boobs from bouncing all over the place; it wasn't meant to show them off.

The office lacked the busy and steady hum during the week, but a few people shuffled around the lobby and voices carried from a few of the open businesses.

I stepped into the copy room, spotting David standing by the huge industrial photocopier and looking at his phone.

Hot fucking damn. Could this kid get any hotter? Dressed in relaxed jeans and a gray short-sleeve Henley shirt that accentuated his muscled and toned arms, he belonged in the pages of a clothing catalog. A golden retriever and a tire swing hanging from a tree would complete the picture-perfect look.

How was it possible for him to look flawlessly sexy in business suits and casual attire? The world was definitely not fair, especially when I wanted to yank his shirt off his sculpted body and then lick –

"Are you done eye fucking me?" David interrupted, with a smirk, as he leaned against the copier with his hands shoved in the front pockets of his jeans.

"Uh, what?" I said, shaking the sexual images from my mind.

"I asked," he said slowly, pushing himself off the machine. "Are you done undressing me with your pretty little eyes?"

Please don't come any closer, I prayed. *Another step, and I will yank my yoga pants and panties off in record speed.*

"You think my eyes are pretty?" I asked distractingly, batting my eyelashes.

He shook his head, waving his index finger at me. "Don't avoid the question, Cat."

My heart jumped excitedly at the way he said my name. Seductively. Purposefully. All the cute flirting made my reproductive organs ache for attention.

"Was it this pose that made you all hot and bothered?" David asked, slouching a bit and running his fingers through his beautiful dark blonde locks in slow motion.

He gave me a serious pissed off look.

I furrowed my eyebrows. "What are you doing?"

"Giving you my best sultry look."

I laughed for a good solid ten seconds. "You look mad."

David pretended to pout and scanned the room. He took a few steps backward, crunching copy paper under his feet, and leaned against the wall. Holding his head high, he bent one leg back so that one of his sneakered feet pressed against the white wall.

"You look awkward," I said, rolling my eyes.

"This isn't sexy?"

I shook my head.

"What about this?"

Still leaning against the wall, David crossed his ankles and folded his arms against his chest – the ultimate senior picture pose.

"Sorry, kid," I said, shrugging. "I don't think modeling is in the cards for you."

David sighed in faux defeat and pushed himself off the wall. I looked around the usually meticulously clean copy room, which was now a disaster area. Different-sized pieces of paper, crumpled or ripped, littered the floor. The lid of the photocopier stood upright, and all the drawers were pulled out with paper stuffed haphazardly.

My eyes widened in horror at the carnage, and David held up his hands in defense.

"Cat, I can explain," he said slowly and softly.

"How? Could? You?" I asked, emphasizing each word for mock dramatic purposes.

"I'm so sorry."

I launched myself at him and lightly pounded my fists on his hard chest. "Why?" I pretended to sob. "Why?"

"It didn't mean anything, Cat," he said, grabbing my wrists and holding them against his body.

Feeling his heart beat stirred something inside me.

"You knew she was my best friend, David."

"I know. It just … just happened," he said, gently running his knuckles down my cheek and resting one hand on the small of my back. "She wouldn't stop beeping at me. I tried to ignore her. I really did, but … but I couldn't resist playing with the buttons on her control panel."

My breath caught in my throat as David slowly twirled a strand of my hair around his finger. When his piercing green eyes searched mine, I was pretty sure I stopped breathing altogether. Our faces, our lips were so damn close; the charade felt very much real.

I wasn't sure who broke the moment first, but we both took a giant step away from each other and awkwardly chuckled to fill the silence.

"Well, that got weird real fast," he said, running a hand behind his neck and pretending to read some of fliers tacked to the huge bulletin board.

"Uh, yeah," I agreed, tucking a few loose strands behind my ears. "Um, so what happened here?"

"One of the other interns, Collin, called me in a panic this morning because he forgot to make these special presentation packets for a meeting first thing on Monday. He conveniently remembered during his drive to Chicago last night."

"That is very convenient," I agreed sarcastically.

"I kinda thought shoving some papers into a machine wouldn't be that hard."

"And what lesson did you learn?"

"That machines have feelings too?" he answered sheepishly.

I snickered and shook my head in amusement.

"So yeah, I kinda got a little angry when the copier shut down on me."

"A little angry?" I raised an eyebrow in disbelief.

"Okay, I was really angry. Oh, before I forget, you're special order, mi'lady."

He bowed dramatically, presenting me with my beautifully delicious-looking blended coffee drink.

"Come here, beautiful," I cooed, taking the drink from his hand and swirling the contents around with the straw.

"You've got a coffee problem, you know that, right?" David asked, his eyes sweeping over my running outfit.

"Shut your face," I snarled teasingly.

He chuckled. "So, you still run?"

I set my drink aside and inspected the photocopier. "Yeah. I eat too much and drink too much coffee. What about you? Do you still run?"

"Yeah," he said, picking up the papers from the floor. "Not as much as I should, but I still enjoy it."

"Didn't you run on the varsity team your sophomore year?" I asked, restacking a ream of paper in a tray.

"Yeah, I ran a few varsity races. Coach Banning wanted to see how some of the sophomores competed in a faster race."

"You were good," I said, closing the drawers. "You and some other kids in your grade were good runners."

"I can't believe you remember that," David said, stuffing some papers into a big blue confidential shred bin. "Yeah, we were cocky little shits on the junior varsity team."

I laughed, grabbing a few fliers from the bulletin board for a test run.

"Reality hit us hard when we ran our first varsity race," he admitted, shaking his head. "Definitely a faster pace than JV."

David and I spent the majority of the time reminiscing about certain cross country meets and other runners as we cleaned up the copy room, fixed the photocopier that we decided to name Veronica, and started assembling twenty-five packets.

I tossed my empty cup in the recycling bin as David waited for the remaining copies to finish printing.

"Oh hey, Gail's stopping by for a day or two next week. We should all hang out sometime," he said hesitantly.

Even an unlimited supply of my favorite coffee couldn't make my smile stay once my mind registered his words.

"Rumor has it you're really good with your mouth, kitty cat," Marty Pullman had whispered disgustingly in my ear as I switched books at my locker between classes.

"What?" I had asked, confused a senior basketball player was talking to me and irritated at him for standing in my way.

"You know," he had smirked, glancing down at his package.

I stupidly followed his gaze.

"Fuck off," I had hissed, stepping back and slamming the locker door closed.

Marty grabbed my arm, roughly pushing me against the row of lockers and trapping me with his tall athletic body. We probably looked like a couple trying to cop a feel between classes.

"Come on, kitty," he purred creepily, pressing his body against mine. "We could be good together."

With my heart racing at an alarming rate, I kneed him in the junk as hard as I could. As soon as he doubled over in pain, I shot off without looking back or even paid attention to students I accidentally bumped into. I remembered his words echoing in the hallway, "Fucking bitch!"

"Cat?" David repeated, with a serious frown. "Are you okay?"

"Uh, yeah," I stammered, slowly inching my way toward the door. "I, uh, need to get going."

"Give me a sec to clean up here, and I can drive you home."

I shook my head anxiously. "It's okay. I like to run. I'll see you later. Good luck on Monday."

After my clumsy word vomit, I took off and ignored his calls after me as my lungs demanded fresh air and my mind begged for clarity. I was a fucking fool for believing I could simply ignore his relation to his stupid sister. Even the mere mention of her name threw me back to a time I never ever wanted to revisit.

I ran home in record time, knowing distance and time alone would give me some peace of mind. My resolve to stop hanging out with David strengthened as hot water pelted my skin in the shower. Glass after glass of chilled sweet white wine gave me courage to ignore David's numerous texts. He was seriously the last person I wanted to talk to about the one person I never wanted to think about again – or ever.

Unfortunately, my liquid courage and my steely resolve vanished the moment I stepped into work Monday. As the complete chicken shit I was, I successfully dodged David for two days by eating lunch at my desk and rerouting my coffee runs to the café's dining section.

"Out of sight out of mind" became my mantra. My awful high school memories couldn't haunt me if David wasn't around to remind me of her.

I almost marked the third day a success when I made my final coffee run. Glancing longingly at a beautiful triple chocolate cupcake in the display case, I felt the heat of his damn presence behind me in line. He didn't even need to cough or say a damn word for my stupid horny body to recognize his.

Straightening my back immediately and forcing my eyes to stare vacantly at the drink menu hanging behind the counter, I remained silent.

"You're avoiding me," David said in a low and even tone.

Nice deduction skills, Captain Obvious, I thought sarcastically.

As I sucked in a deep breath, his light masculine scent tested every ounce of my willpower to keep my eyes on the chalkboard menu. One look at his stupid handsome face with his sharp cheekbones would melt my defenses. One glance at his impeccable clothes and physique would steer my mind into sexual overdrive.

"I've been busy," I said casually, throwing in a small shoulder shrug for good measure.

"Bullshit, Cat." His warm breath tickled my ear and neck.

I wasn't sure if I needed to suppress a moan or a giggle.

He sighed deeply as I took a step forward when the line shuffled.

"Would you feel better if you knew I don't like my sister either?"

Yes! A million times yes, my stupid heart sang out.

"Maybe," I said shortly.

"Can we please talk? After work? There's a bar nearby."

Nope, my mind said stubbornly, knowing my resolve would dissolve to absolutely nothing if I spent any time with him.

Even if David didn't like her, Gail was still his sister. Nothing could ever change that.

"Please, Cat," he begged softly with a hint of sadness.

"Okay," I agreed reluctantly, wondering why I couldn't say no.

Even though meeting him outside of work was a terrible idea for so many reasons, my curiosity about their fractured relationship was stronger.

My curiosity might not kill me but it could definitely lead me into trouble.

The bar David chose wasn't the usual hangout for interns, giving us a chance to talk without interruptions. Arriving first, he grabbed a booth near the back and polished off half his beer by the time I slid into the well-worn brown vinyl seat across from him.

Our awkward staring contest didn't last long when the server promptly dropped by to take our drink order. Sighing deeply, he ran a hand through his already disheveled locks as I noticed the faint bags under his eyes and the tired and defeated look. My heart ached slightly at his miserable appearance.

"Cat, I know my sister isn't the nicest person," David started hesitantly.

A mix of a sarcastic chuckle and disbelieving snort burst from my lips. I mouthed a silent apology to the server who cast me a worried frown as she delivered our pints of beer.

I seriously believed Gail couldn't be sincerely nice to anyone even if her life depended on it.

"In all honesty, I haven't seen her for over a year. We haven't had a real conversation until a week ago."

I sipped my beer, waiting for him to continue.

"I stopped talking to her after she slept with a guy our mom started dating," David admitted, slowly rotating his first glass pint in his hands.

Holy shit! This girl is still bat-shit crazy.

"Oh," I replied softly, not knowing what to say.

"Our parents divorced when I was eleven," he continued, without emotion, as his eyes stared vacantly at the table. "He admitted to cheating on our mom several times. I stayed with my mom because we were close anyway. And I was severely pissed off with my dad. Gail chose to live with him."

"I'm sorry," I offered sincerely. "That's a lot for an 11-year-old to deal with."

David shrugged. "I haven't talked to my dad in years because he's never apologized for his affairs. He thinks money fixes everything, giving me cash on my birthday or any major occasion. But I never kept any of it, sent it all back to him."

With a heavy sigh, he swallowed the remainder of his first beer. "Anyway, my mom started dating a nice guy last year, and for whatever reason, Gail slept with him. But what surprised me the most was my mom's impassive reaction when she told me. Like she kinda expected this to happen."

Maybe giving birth to a demon baby gave her super powers, I thought, trying to remember if I had seen his mom at a cross country meet. *Oh, Cat, that was just dumb. Demon baby doesn't even sound that vile. Soul-sucking succubus?*

"How did your mom find out?" I asked as a plausible explanation formed in my mind.

"Uh, um, she caught them in her bed," David mumbled, shifting uncomfortably. "The classic cheating scenario."

"Why did Gail choose to live with your dad?"

"Because she knew Dad would give her anything she wanted. And she and Mom didn't have the greatest relationship."

"She couldn't manipulate your mom," I guessed, cutting to the real reason.

Squaring back his broad shoulders with surprise, he nodded. "They argued all the time before the divorce. Gail even blamed her for Dad's affairs."

I refrained from rolling my eyes, knowing my bitter attitude wouldn't help him. "Before the incident, were they close?"

David shook his head.

"I think Gail wanted your mom to catch them because she wanted to see how badly she hurt your mom."

"Cat, I don't know," he said, with a frown. "My sister may have issues, but I don't think she's that diabolical."

Diabolical! So much better than demon baby. Diabolical gremlin?

I leaned back against the booth and shrugged indifferently. If David doubted my highly probable theory, then that was his problem not mine. Convincing him otherwise wasn't my job.

I had no doubt Gail made their mom's life hell in other ways over the years. But nothing could take down a woman's self esteem faster than catching a boyfriend in bed with a much younger woman.

"I get you guys didn't get along in high school – " he started to protest.

"I have no fucking clue what I did to make her hate me so much," I interrupted angrily, watching his eye widen at my heated outburst. "She had been more than a bully, David. She knew how to psychologically tear me down."

"Several students and teachers witnessed you physically assaulting Martin Pullman," the principal had calmly told me the next day in his office.

We were sitting at a round wooden table with the head guidance counselor, the head school nurse, the student council staff advisor, and the student council president. Based on the sympathetic and reassuring smiles from the guidance counselor, the school nurse, and the council advisor, I knew I wasn't in trouble for kicking Marty in the gonads.

"Mr. Vallen, the student council president, also confirmed with at least a dozen students regarding a rumor leading up to the incident," the principal had continued, glancing at me without judgment. "We've also spoken with Mr. Pullman and his parents, and Mr. Pullman took responsibility for the incident and would like to apologize to you."

I shook my head furiously, grateful the nurse sitting next to me reached over and gently squeezed my hand.

"I figured you would not be comfortable with his presence, Ms. Coleman," the principal had said, noting my terrified reaction. "Mr. Pullman has specific instructions to not approach you for the remainder of the year. He has also been dismissed from the basketball team and is currently suspended for the rest of the week."

The damage had already been done. The idea of dating fucking terrified me, especially when any of the varsity jocks made obscene gestures or crude remarks in my direction. I never stepped outside my circle of friends, preferring to attend dances and other events with my girlfriends instead of a date.

The small amount of confidence I had had been severely battered. Even under the protective eyes from teachers and other staff, I no longer felt safe. I kept my head down, focused on school and cross country, and worked on escaping my hometown as soon as I possibly could.

"Cat," he said gently, with worry flickering in his eyes.

I took a deep breath to calm my nerves and then gulped down half my beer.

"You weren't her only target," David revealed. "She made my life hell except I was too young and stupid to know at the time. She constantly flirted with my friends when I was in junior high. I stupidly thought she was being nice until I realized more and more guys wanted to be my friend."

Remaining silent and finishing the rest of my drink, I thought about Angelique Ferris and her overwhelming sense of humiliation. Not surprisingly her relationship with Gail's ex-boyfriend didn't last long after the talent show fiasco. Angelique transferred to a different school the following year.

"Again, I was young and really stupid," he repeated, with a resigned sigh. "We were never really close because she was always off doing her own thing with her friends. But, for whatever reason, I always stood up for her. She's my sister."

I had grown up believing siblings should always look out for one another. My conviction was destroyed when my sisters chose to believe the rumors over my truth.

"We grew up believing family comes first," I said bitterly.

"Yeah, but all that goes to shit when a dad puts his dick before his family."

I empathized with David's disdain for his dad because I knew what it felt like to have parents turn their back on a kid who had adored them for so long.

After almost draining his second pint, he set the glass on the table and gave me a cute little half smile. "Gail called a month ago and said she's changed."

Oh hell no. Another chuckle slash snort flew my lips, and I quickly clapped a hand over my mouth.

My gut reaction over her alleged change of heart was so strong that I would name my firstborn daughter after her if I was wrong. But I wasn't. I seriously wasn't.

David smirked at me. "Yeah, that was my first reaction too."

My heart skipped a small beat as I bit my lower lip.

"She's been seeing this guy for about six months now. Says she's in love."

Nope, I thought, relaxing my face to hide the tremendous amount of doubt.

In no particular order, Gail loved herself, money, and attention. I seriously doubted she could love another person.

"The guy – some lawyer – lives about thirty minutes away from here," he said. "She's visiting him now, but we plan to meet for dinner tomorrow night."

"Do you believe her?" I asked hesitantly.

Desperation clawed inside me because I liked him more than I really should. Even if the she-devil truly changed and genuinely apologized a million times, the memories of what she did would never be forgotten.

David shrugged, running a finger up and down the side of his glass. "Honestly? I dunno. I want to give her the benefit of the doubt."

"What does your mom think?"

"She said everyone deserves a second chance."

Worst advice ever, I thought sullenly, hating the very vague answer.

"So, what are you gonna do?" I asked, knowing I wasn't going to like his reply.

"She's my sister, Cat," he said, with a soft frustrated sigh. "I should at least hear her out, right?"

Absolutely fucking not, my mind yelled stubbornly.

I shook my head. "You're asking the wrong person, David."

As much as I wanted him to tell his sister to go to hell, I didn't have the right to tell anyone what to do when it came to family. And I certainly had no right to make David choose between me and Gail.

"I kinda invited you because I thought a third person would make things less awkward," he admitted sheepishly. "I didn't mean to upset you. I'm really sorry."

Sucking in a deep breath and slowly exhaling it, I said evenly, "I'm not going to apologize for not liking or even not trusting your sister after all the stuff she did."

"What did she do?"

"I don't want to talk about it." I shook my head as if that could stop the memories from surfacing.

Did he simply ignore the rumors or stories about his sister and her wicked ways back then? I didn't expect him to know what she wrote in my senior yearbook, but he had to know about the time Gail "accidentally" tripped and spilled her lunch of spaghetti and meatballs on my favorite pale pink sweater. The incident taught me to keep spare clothes in my locker and never wear anything expensive to school.

"Gail, uh, mentioned her best friend, Annalise, was gonna come with her but she, um, backed out," David said nervously, swallowing the last of his beer.

I raised an eyebrow at his sudden anxious state.

"Annalise and I were together for about two years," he explained, noticing my curiosity. "She and Gail were roommates their freshman year in college. She often came home with Gail whenever our dad was out of town. They would throw huge parties, and, of course, my friends wanted to go. Long story short, Annalise and I started dating after I graduated from high school, but we broke up when I decided to move here for school."

A ton of questions flooded my mind. Was he still in love with Annalise? Did she still love him? Why did she bail on the trip? Did she wrap her probably long and perfect legs around his naked waist as he probably nuzzled her slender neck and whispered sweet words in her ear? I hated her already.

"No hard feelings between the two of you?" I asked as casually as possible.

I wanted to pat myself on the back for asking an "adult" question instead of blatantly blurting out, "Why did you guys break up? Do you still love her? What happened?"

David shook his head. "We just sorta drifted apart even though she was only an hour away at school. The breakup was mutual."

The majority of my relationships usually ended with tears, ice cream, and lame wishes at 11:11 p.m.

"Gail thought we were the perfect couple. I think she was more heartbroken than we were."

If only she had a heart to break, I thought cheekily before wondering if he had been the perfect boyfriend.

Did he like to hold hands in public? Did he like to cuddle in bed? Was he the type to send birthday flowers? Did he even remember important dates? Was he the type to remember little things like order extra whipped cream on a blended coffee drink?

"I'm kinda glad Annalise backed out because Gail probably would've focused her attention on getting us back together."

"No chance at reconciliation?" The stupid words slipped from my mouth before my mind even had a chance to process the question.

I wasn't even sure I wanted to know the answer even though my chest twitched a teeny bit in anticipation.

Beer caused heartburn, right?

David shook his head, giving me a small impish smile. "We're honestly just friends. We talk every now and then."

I frowned slightly as an unnecessary wave of relief washed through me at the prospect of him remaining emotionally unattached to an ex-girlfriend.

"So," he started hesitantly, rotating the empty glass in his hands. "Are we okay? I'm really sorry I upset you."

"Yeah," I said, with a timid smile. "We're okay."

A smaller wave of relief surged through me because ignoring his texts and dodging him over the past few days had been exhausting. I missed having lunch on the outdoor patio and reading my book.

Awkward silence fell between us as we simply looked at each other. A huge sigh escaped my chest when his phone screen lit up and his eyes darted over it to read the message.

"A couple of guys I work with are hanging out at a different bar nearby. Wanna join them?"

I shook my head. "Thanks for the invite, but I should get going."

"I'll walk out with you," David offered, scooting out of the booth to pay the bill at the bar.

As soon as I stepped outside, my eyes fluttered closed for a moment as my skin welcomed the coolness of the summer air. I hoped my favorite bottle of wine at home would lessen the sting of disappointment swimming inside my chest.

Life was so unfair, I thought miserably.

My crush would remain a crush. David was a good guy who would always remain loyal to the two most important women in his life – his mom and his stupid mean girl of a sister.

"Thanks for the beer," I said as he joined me on the sidewalk.

Shoving his hands into his pockets, he simply nodded and slightly hunched his broad shoulders together. His obvious uncertainty about what to say or possibly even do next made him look adorable. I held back from tucking myself into his tall, muscular frame and wrapping my arms around him.

Ugh. Life was so fucking unfair.

"Where did you park? I'll walk you to your car," David said finally, blowing out a deep breath.

"I parked in the ramp," I said, nodding my head in the general direction. "I'll be fine. Go meet your friends."

"My mom taught me to always open the door and walk a woman to her car, especially at night."

The pride in his voice subtly expressed how much love and respect he had for the woman who raised him to be a gentleman. I completely blamed his dad for creating the evil monster.

"David, seriously, I'll be fine," I said, with an eye roll and a huff.

"Sorry, but my mom didn't raise a savage. Unless you want to join me?" he asked, making his eyes go wide and sticking out his lower lip dramatically. I giggled and shook my head. "Come on. It'll be fun. Drink beer. Throw darts. Accidentally throw darts at some assholes."

My ears and eyes perked up at the word "darts". My college girlfriends and I perfected the skill with hot guys who loved showing hot girls how to throw a dart. I was lumped into the "hot girl" group by default because my roommate and her girlfriend were spectacularly gorgeous.

"Darts, eh?" David said, noting my sudden interest. "Come on, Cat. All the games on me."

Free rounds of darts was somewhere on my long list of weaknesses.

Despite us "being good," I couldn't avoid him for the rest of his summer internship. My overactive fantasies to blindfold him with his tie or lick whipped cream off his muscled chest would fade over time, right? I really didn't need him to fulfill the ache between my legs when I had my vivid imagination and trusty vibrator.

I needed to figure out how to remain friends with him anyway. Now was a good time as any to start, right? At a bar. Over a few games of darts. With his co-workers. Perfectly harmless fun.

"Okay," I agreed as my fingers twitched with anticipation of holding a dart.

"Yes!" He shouted triumphantly, pumping his arms over his head before throwing punches at an imaginary boxing opponent.

I laughed and shook my head as I started walking down the block to the second bar. "You're a dummy."

"Yeah, but I'm your dummy," he teased, easily catching up with me in a few long strides, as his hands swiped across my waist.

Stop! My mind screamed, with panic. *You can't be "just friends" with this dummy. Run to your car right now! Run!*

With my body reeling from the scorch of his faint and quick touch, it begged for more contact no matter how small or meaningless. As a result, my resolve to keep our friendship platonic needed to be stronger. So much stronger.

Pixie Star was a low-key bar with about half dozen regulars sitting at the counter and chatting with the bartenders. Round high-top tables and stools filled the rest of the small space. Two well-used coin-operated dartboards stood against the wall by the end of the bar toward the back.

I was well familiar with the place, hanging out with fellow interns last year after a brutal day in the office. Pitchers of beer were cheap, and the dartboards absorbed our frustrations with every throw.

As we approached two guys, both sporting dress pants, button down shirts with the sleeves rolled, and loosened ties, David casually placed a hand on my back and introduced me to two architects, Xander and Ben.

While David fed quarters into one of the machines, Xander, a tall handsome guy with dark chocolate skin and beautifully bald, winked at me and handed me a set of three red darts.

"Ladies, first," David said, making a sweeping motion toward the throwing line.

"Thank you," I said politely but added with a hint of arrogance. "Be prepared for an ass kicking, gentlemen."

I ignored the snickers as I carefully lined up my shot. A second later, I threw the first dart – landing on triple 20 – and without too much thought, I hurled the other two darts, hitting a single 19 and the outer bullseye.

"Aw, shit, guys," Xander hollered as I pulled the darts from the board. "Gotta professional now!"

I walked back to the table with a confident smirk and boldly winked at David, but the kid winked back with the same amount of swagger.

Breathe, Cat, I reminded myself. *We're just having fun. Nothing but harmless fun.*

"This is Team Greenland's last shot, ladies and gentlemen," Xander mimicked quietly as a fake sports announcer. "If Ms. Coleman hits a single 2, Team Greenland takes the win, but if her dart lands anywhere else, Team USA still has a shot at claiming the world title."

"Greenlaw. Greenland. Not very creative with team names," David interrupted sarcastically.

The first-year architect shrugged his broad muscular shoulders. "I didn't hear your brilliant ideas."

"I don't like the fact my team is named after the weakest player," I added sourly, focusing on my last shot at the toe line.

Xander and Ben hooted with amusement and playfully punched David in the shoulders.

I took careful aim and threw the dart, landing on a single two and effectively winning the game.

David and I immediately screamed with joy. As my arms automatically shot up in the air, he grabbed my waist, lifting me off the ground, and spun around several times.

Dizzy from the thrill of winning.

Dizzy from his burning touch.

Dizzy from the room spinning around.

I wrapped my arms around David's neck to keep myself balanced.

As soon as my feet touched the floor and my body released from his embrace, Xander swooped in and swung me around for a few seconds.

With his eyebrows furrowed, David asked, "What are you doing? Why are you celebrating our win?"

He shrugged, flashing him a good-natured smile, as his hand lingered on my back until I regained my balance. "I dunno. Twirling her around looked like fun."

I giggled, removing my hand from his shoulder, as the dizziness faded.

"Yeah, but that wasn't a twirl," Ben pointed out, with a soft Spanish accent that made me swoon. "You guys were spinning her around not twirling."

With naturally tan skin, deep hazel eyes, and a shaved head, Ben showed me pictures of his gorgeous girlfriend and their adorable cats, Baby and Johnny, when we weren't throwing darts. I suspected he talked incessantly about "his girl" because I probably appeared too eager to listen to anything he said.

When words like "mi amor" or "idiotas estúpidos" fell from Ben's lips, I wondered if David was fluent in a second language. I would haul his tight little ass into the bathroom so fast and have my wicked way with him if he spoke any language other than German.

Accents were at the top of my weakness list. Watching a show or movie with any Brits running around was damn near impossible without me getting turned on at some point.

"What's the difference?" Xander asked curiously, feeding more quarters in the machine for another round.

After grabbing my hand, Ben lifted his arm and I smoothly danced under it as if I was a pretty ballerina.

"That's a twirl," he said matter-of-factly.

David rolled his eyes, and Xander pointed an accusing finger at me. "You were a distraction. With your longs legs and perfect hair."

"Nice try," I said dryly, making a circular motion with my index finger. "Being devastatingly handsome and tall also requirements to work at the firm? I mean, seriously, is 'model looks required' stated somewhere on the application?"

"You think I'm tall?" Ben asked, puffing out his chest with pride. He stood a good inch taller than me.

"You think I'm devastatingly handsome?" David teased, holding a hand over his heart.

I looked at Ben, giving him an "eh" shrug. He deflated his chest and hunched his shoulder dramatically to appear heartbroken.

Tapping an index finger to my chin, I studied David as if I was a recruiter for a modeling agency. "Well, I'm sure there's some exceptions to the rules."

He covered his face with both hands and pretended to dramatically sob. Xander turned the distance between the dartboards and the throwing line into his personal runway, strutting back and forth, and posed for imaginary cameras.

"You could learn a few things from him," I told David as we watched his co-worker sashay off the fake runway. "He's a natural."

Tilting his head slightly, his breath feathered over my ear as he whispered huskily, "I'm a natural in other areas."

Holy fucking shit! The hysterical part of my brain screamed as a small shiver ran down my spine. *Kick off your heels, hike up your cute little pencil skirt, and run away from this guy as far and as fast as you fucking can!*

Shit, man, the logical part of my brain sighed with resignation. *Why did he have to take it there? Why?*

"Definitely not a natural with photocopiers and darts," I teased, lightly nibbling on one of my fingernails. "So, I wonder what it could be."

Grabbing the darts from Xander's out-stretched palm, I tossed a confident sway in my hips as I approached the toe line and expertly chucked the first dart at the bullseye.

"I'm on Cat's team!" Xander shouted as the other two darts landed on high-scoring areas. "Fuckin' dibs!"

Ben muttered something in Spanish, and David scoffed in protest. I simply smirked to myself as I grabbed the darts from the board. This was definitely more fun than drinking my favorite bottle of wine while watching TV at home, but it still wasn't the wisest idea.

The guys and I spilled out of the bar after a revised Team USA claimed the world title and Team Greenland paid for the tab.

"You're welcome to play darts with us anytime," Ben said, with a huge smile, swinging an arm around my shoulder and pulling close me.

"Thanks," I said, returning the smile. "I had a really good time."

"Benny!" Xander hollered as he slapped David on the back a few times. "I'm hungry. Let's go grab a burger. You coming, Cat?"

I shook my head, glancing at my watch. "I gotta go. Some of us actually work."

"We work!" Ben cried out, with mock indignation.

"Designing the most phallic buildings isn't work."

"Hey," Xander protested. "It takes time and creativity to design the best one."

"And a certain amount of stealth," David added jokingly. "Boss can't know we're wasting our God-given talents."

"I wouldn't say God-given," I muttered, with a sly wink.

A sense of pride warmed me as the guys laughed and joked around a bit more.

"Ready, Cat?" David asked, with an expression I couldn't quite read, as he held out his hand for me.

My eyes carefully studied his steady palm for a brief moment before reluctantly accepting. A subtle gasp drifted through my lips as his fingers perfectly laced through mine. No need for adjustments. No fingers awkwardly colliding. Just a simple connection that made my heart sing with so much damn happiness.

We remained silent as we walked toward the parking ramp, content to watch other people stumble out of other bars and listen to the steady hum of traffic. After tightening his grip on my hand as we crossed a busy street, David stopped suddenly in the middle of the empty sidewalk and turned to gaze at me.

My eyes narrowed in confusion as I noticed a look of contemplation on his handsome face. Just as I parted my lips to ask him if something was wrong, his beautiful mouth slowly descended on mine. My eyelids fluttered closed on their own accord as the warmth and tenderness of the kiss ignited a flame in my belly.

His free hand cradled the back of my head as his tongue smoothly invaded my mouth.

Holy shit, the kid's a fucking natural.

The sexy as fuck kiss alone made me hunger for more. Made me crave him. As his fingers tangled in my hair, the sound of a car horn blaring longer than necessary pulled us apart.

"Get a room!" some guy from one of the passing cars yelled out the window.

"We will!" I shouted back unapologetically as David tugged on my hand to resume our silent walk.

As my lips tingled spectacularly from our first kiss, dozens of red flags waved furiously in my mind. I sure as hell didn't trust Gail or her claim to have changed. But did I trust David? Should I trust him?

I tried pulling my hand from his when we approached my dark blue four-door sedan, but his grasp remained firm.

Why the fuck was Gail his sister? Why did I like him so much?

Clutching the slender strap of my small black purse as if it would save me from drowning, I stared at the cracked pavement beneath my feet.

"David, we shouldn't – " I said nervously.

"I won't let her hurt you," he interrupted softly, lifting my chin with two fingers. "I promise."

All my defenses crashed in seconds when I saw nothing but the truth in his piercing green eyes.

While the logical part of my brain continued to wave red flags around, my heart skipped excitedly at the idea of newfound feels. The beginning stage of something new. The giddy anticipation of reading a new text or seeing him again. The wandering thoughts of what could happen next.

The last time those feelings struck me was when I started dating Jonah Eversman during my third year in college. The gorgeous business major never failed to make my stomach ache from laughing so much whenever we ran into each other at the bars. Even though the sexual spark burned brightly between us, we somehow lost the deeper connection that attracted us in the first place.

While I wanted to ignore it, I couldn't deny the lingering connection between David and I. The physical attraction was obvious, but something deeper pulled me toward him.

Fuck it. I stepped closer and lifted our still entwined hands between us because the dumbass refused to let go. However, my knees buckled slightly when his lips softly grazed my knuckles.

"Kiss me, David," I whispered because everything in me wanted more.

His free hand immediately cupped the back of my neck as his lips hungrily crashed onto mine. This kiss was explosive. Hot. Demanding. And it was so fucking good. Damn, the kid really was a natural at the kissing game.

When a content sigh escaped from my throat, he finally dropped my hand and dug his fingers into my waist. My free hand latched onto his solid bicep in case my knees decided to give out.

A shudder ran through my body as his tongue deftly explored my mouth and I tasted a hint of beer and salted popcorn. My fingers on his arm reached for his shoulder before winding up at the nape. Just as I slightly tugged on a few strands, an erotic groan rumbled from deep within his chest.

His body gently pushed mine against my car as the kiss deepened into dangerous territory. The area where I didn't give a damn about the ramp's security cameras catching me throw David on his back on the hood of my car and then mount him like a koala bear in heat.

Fortunately, the sound of squealing tires rounding a corner somewhere in the structure prevented me from fulfilling one of my public sex fantasies.

"Fuck," David muttered, pulling back and scrubbing a hand down his face.

My trembling fingers frantically dove into my purse in search of the car keys as my lowered eyes caught a silver car rolling by.

"So, um," I stalled nervously, opening the door and tossing my purse onto the passenger seat. "I'll see you tomorrow."

My aching body and the logical part of my brain bickered about the next move. Horny little Cat wanted to drag David into the back seat of my car, hike up my skirt, and ride him like a drunk girl on a mechanical bull. And logical and sensible Cat wanted to say goodbye and then race home to use my vibrator until I passed from several intense orgasms.

"I had a good time tonight," he said in a lowered tone, providing Horny Cat with a reason to follow through with her wicked plan.

"Me too," I squeaked out because my muddled mind couldn't form a coherent thought if my life depended on it.

Grinning devilishly, David picked up my hand and gently kissed my knuckles. "I'll see you tomorrow."

I nodded before opening the door and scrambling inside.

He waved before shoving his hands in the front pockets of his pants and walking toward his car.

I caught my giddy reflection in the rearview mirror and sighed heavily in shame.

Harmless fun my ass.

"Hey, champ," David teased, setting his lunch tray on the table and plopping into an empty seat next to me.

My plan to play totally cool vanished at the sight of him and his irresistible grin. I never stood a chance, especially when he was dressed in form-fitting navy blue slacks, a white blue-striped button down shirt, and navy blue tie. Even after three rounds with my vibrator last night, Horny Cat wanted to drag him to the parking ramp and cross off "car sex" on my bucket sex list.

"Grasshopper," I replied, blushing slightly at the naughty image in my mind.

"Xander and Ben are already arguing about teams for next time."

I snickered, closing the book I had been reading before David arrived.

"Are you doing anything this weekend?" he asked casually, watching me finish the rest of my third cup of coffee.

I simply shrugged, unable to meet his gaze. Hanging out – hell, even flirting – with him at work kept me safe because the professional in me wouldn't do anything stupid to jeopardize my job. Seeing him outside of the office was a completely different story because my logic had very little to no power over my impulsive side.

"Hey," David said softly, sensing my hesitancy. "I meant what I said last night. I won't let her hurt you."

I really wish I could believe that, I thought sadly.

"She's your sister," I said flatly. "She's trying to make amends."

"I'm not even sure if I can even forgive her for what she did to our mom."

I shook my head. "I'm not worth the complication."

"Cat." Even with his tone low, the way he almost growled my name was a simple command, telling me to listen carefully. "You're not a complication."

I opened my mouth to protest when his warm hand covered mine.

"You're not a complication," David repeated seriously, his green eyes boring into mine. "You're my clarity."

The corners of my mouth lifted into a small smile as I thought, *That's one of my favorite songs.*

As my mind greedily accepted the simple statement as a positive sign, a familiar female voice calling David's name served a really, really bad omen.

Turning our heads slightly, we watched his sister, Gail, walk excitedly toward our table.

In the five years since high school graduation, the bitch hadn't aged one bit. Shoulder length pale blonde hair bounced perfectly with each step; blue evil eyes narrowed on her prey; and rail thin figure without an ounce of fat accentuated in ripped skinny jeans and lacy gray camisole. She still looked like pure evil but without the skanky cheerleader uniform.

"Davey!" She threw herself into her younger brother's arms when he stood up, and he hugged her awkwardly for a second before pulling back.

"What are you doing here, Gail?" he asked, frowning. "I thought we were meeting for dinner tonight."

"I thought I'd surprise my baby brother. It's been so long since we've seen each other, and I wanted to spend some time with you."

"I wish you would've called or texted me," David said stiffly, glancing at me nervously.

Gail pretended to pout, slightly sticking out her plump lower lip, and lightly punched him in the shoulder. "That's no fun."

Her dangerous blue eyes curiously followed his anxious gaze on me and flickered with genuine surprise at seeing another familiar face.

"Kitty Cat?" she exclaimed incredulously.

The nickname honestly never annoyed me. With a name like Cat, any terms or sounds associated with felines was basically an open invitation to anyone with small and unimaginative minds.

Right then, I knew I spared my firstborn daughter a name I would forever associate with evil because Gail was the still same.

It was the casual sound of her voice. It was the clever tone. It was her presence. It was *her*.

She might have fooled everyone around her. But not me. I still recognized the diabolical witch from high school.

"Hey," I said, with a cold smile, as I stood up and grabbed my lunch tray. My appetite immediately vanished the moment I heard her pretentious voice. "Sorry, but I gotta run. I'll see you later."

Maybe it was the third cup of coffee I had just drained or my choice to wear one of my favorite outfits – a light gray short sleeve dress with a white collar and black pumps – that gave me the courage to quickly and lightly press my lips to his cheek.

"Text me later," I purred and walked boldly past his sister with my head held high.

"Miss Goody Goody hasn't changed at all." I heard Gail whine haughtily.

"Knock it off," David snapped.

That's right, you dumb bitch, I thought irritatingly. *Some people don't ever fucking change.*

The logical part of my mind and my annoyingly overactive imagination clashed for the remainder of the day.

My sensibilities instructed me to calm down and trust David and his feelings for me. Gail would disappear after having dinner with him, and then he and I could resume whatever we were doing in the first place. Maybe we could actually go on a first date.

But my overactive imagination simply threw any and all logic out the fucking window as it created so many mock scenarios and conversations between the brother and sister duo.

"Why did you bully Cat in high school?" David would ask innocently.

"What?" Gail would exclaim, with fake tears and a quiver in her voice.

"But she said you bullied her."

"I tried to be her friend," his sister would lie convincingly. "Did you know she tried to spill her lunch of spaghetti and meatballs on me? But I stood up for myself and accidentally dumped the tray on her instead."

"I'll never let that wretched girl hurt you ever again, sweet sister," he would promise protectively.

Sometimes I really hated my imagination.

His texts at the end of the night did nothing to squash my creative mind.

David: Sorry about lunch today.

David: She's staying at a hotel tonight in town. Had too much to drink at dinner.

I had no doubt Gail could probably drink like a pirate with a wooden leg, but I suspected she extended her stay when she noticed the obvious attraction between me and her brother. Thinking of ways to mess with us – more accurately me – intrigued her.

My instincts screamed she was still a narcissistic, arrogant, and self-serving evil bitch, but I had no right to warn David. He needed to discover that on his own.

David: Meet at my car in parking ramp at lunch?

David: I really want to kiss you again.

Of course, he had to share his thought as I slipped into bed with a giddy smile. The thought of kissing him tomorrow and possibly being with him over the weekend had my hand scrambling to find my vibrator in the drawer of my nightstand.

Life Happens Coffee Helps

Why *the fuck am I a sucker for men in ties?* I wondered as my eyes heatedly raked over David's fine form leaning casually against his blue SUV.

I bit my lower lip in excited anticipation as my mind stripped him from his gray dress pants and blue checkered dress shirt. I had never looked so forward to a lunch break in my life as my eyes were practically glued to the digital clock on my computer screen the entire morning.

The clicking sound of my black high heels caught his attention as he glanced up and smiled as if he had just won a million dollars. Pushing himself off the side of his car once I was in arms length, David grabbed my waist, pulling me flush against him, and kissed me hungrily.

I suppressed a squeal of joy, knowing he wanted me as much as I wanted him, as our tongues battled for dominance. This was what I craved since reading his last text of the night. To be near him. To be with him.

A throaty groan rumbled from his mouth as one of his hands fumbled for the door handle to the back seat. As soon as the door opened, David tucked himself inside and pulled me in. After slamming the door shut, I hiked up the skirt of my sleeveless red polka dot dress and straddled his lap as he leaned against the back seat and stretched out long legs.

"Fuck," I moaned in pleasure as his lips nuzzled my neck and his hands roamed my ass over my dress.

I rolled my hips when his erection pressed against my lacy underwear.

"Cat," he groaned as his hands slipped underneath my skirt and gripped my bare ass.

Wrapping my arms around his neck, I pressed my chest against his and whispered in his ear. "Is she gone? Because I fucking want you all fucking weekend, David."

A long, sexy guttural sound escaped from him when I slowly emphasized "all fucking weekend."

"Just one more night," he gasped out as I gently tugged on his earlobe between my teeth and continued to grind my body against his.

One more night? I didn't want to wait another second. *Wait. Why is she staying another night?*

"She wants to catch up with you," he murmured. "Let's do dinner with her tonight."

Nope. Fuck that idea. Goodbye, ladywood.

Sighing heavily with disappointment and irritation, I disentangled my arms from his neck and slipped off his lap to smooth out my dress. From the corner of my eye, I watched David throw his head back, groan, and adjust himself with one hand.

Goodbye, big guy. I really wanted to meet you this weekend.

"Have dinner with us tonight," he repeated, stretching an arm across the back seat, as his fingers lightly caressed my shoulder.

I shook my head as a huge wave of frustration crashed into my chest. "No thank you. I really don't want to talk to her much less have dinner with her."

"She's willing to try." As soon as the words tumbled out of his mouth, he immediately froze in fear. One look at the desperation and panic in his eyes disclosed he knew he made a huge mistake.

I turned to leave, but David quickly grabbed my hand and scooted closer to me, resting his forehead on my bare shoulder.

"I'm sorry, Cat," he said softly. "I didn't mean it. I'm such an idiot."

I closed my eyes as fury coursed through my mind and body.

"I'm sorry," he repeated, squeezing my hand. "We had a good talk last night, and she wants to spend more time with me. Us."

She wants to fucking screw with us. Me.

"All I want … I just want to be with you - alone. This weekend."

You and me both, buddy.

While his words of wanting to spend the weekend with me sounded heavenly, they did nothing to quell the anger rising in me.

"One more day, Cat," David said, lifting his head. "She's supposed to stay with Annalise for a few days, but she's having trouble reaching her."

She's staying to mess with us. Every fiber in my body sensed the diabolical wheels turning in her mind.

"You should go, David," I said sadly.

"Please don't run from me."

"She's your sister, and she's my tormentor."

"Tormentor? Isn't that a little harsh?" He raised an eyebrow in disbelief.

The last thread holding my reserve together completely snapped.

"Fuck you," I said angrily, yanking my hand away from his, and glowered at him. "You have no idea what she did to me for four fucking years."

"She played harmless pranks," he said, with an exasperated huff. "She told me at dinner last night."

"Harmless pranks?" I shrieked as my chest heaved with pure rage. "Are you fucking kidding me? You think writing 'get fucked' in my yearbook was harmless? Or starting the rumor that I love giving blow jobs to the jocks? You think Marty Pullman trying to rub one out on me in school was harmless?"

The horrified look on his face and the sheer terror in his eyes held the truth. These weren't the stories Gail shared with him. Because why would she start telling the truth now?

"She pulled my skirt down in front of an entire class," I spat out as my mind frantically raced through years of old memories. "I wore jeans and a belt every day after that. Did she think 'accidentally' cutting off a chunk of my hair in art class was harmless? Thank God I looked good with a long layered bob.

"This isn't even close to half the shit she and her fucking friends pulled on me and my friends. She fucking preyed on everyone's insecurities, David. To make them feel small and worthless. So, no, tormentor isn't a little harsh."

"Cat," he said hoarsely; his eyes glassy with regret and pity. "I didn't know. I'm so sorry."

"Save it," I snarled, rolling my eyes. "I like you so damn much, but I knew this would happen sooner or later. And I absolutely refuse to let that conniving little bitch walk all over me again. Oh, and for the fucking record, she hasn't changed one bit.

"This is why we won't work. Ever. She will always be your sister, and I will always be a toy for her. So, stay the fuck away from me."

I stormed out of the SUV and slammed the door closed, not giving him a chance to respond.

The firestorm coursing through every cell in my body tempted me to track down Gail and strangle her with my bare hands. Four years of suffering was enough. Five years and distance made me wiser and stronger.

As much as I liked and wanted to be with David, I hated Gail so much more.

David's insensitive remarks replayed in my mind on a continuous loop for the rest of the day. I ignored his apology text he had sent about an hour after I told him to fuck off. For his own safety, I prayed he wouldn't show during my last coffee run. While I didn't regret a single word – even the swear words – in my honest tirade, the same couldn't be said during a potential second round.

My stiff composure relaxed immediately when Xander sauntered in and stood behind me in line. This beautiful man had superior fashion style, wearing a blue striped button down shirt, pink striped bowtie, and gray dress pants.

"Holy shit, Cat," he said in a lowered voice. "What the hell happened between you two? This morning, the kid looked like he could conquer the world. And after lunch, he looked like the world nearly trampled him to death."

While I figured Xander and Ben noticed our attraction, did they know all the details? What exactly did guys tell each other anyway?

"I told him a relationship could never work between us," I admitted, frowning at the ounce of sadness sneaking into my heart.

"Why?" he asked curiously but then shook his head. "Never mind. It's not my business. But, Cat, you gotta know the kid is in love with you."

I snorted and wrinkled my eyebrows in complete disbelief. Sure, David and I knew each other years ago, but we weren't exactly friends considering the two-year age difference. The minor gap didn't matter now, but it made a difference to a bunch of kids with different priorities and circle of friends.

The cynic in me certainly didn't believe in love at first sight, and it sincerely doubted a person could fall through casual lunches and coffee runs during a three-week period.

"Okay," Xander huffed out reluctantly. "He might not be in love with you, but he's crazy about you. I have never seen an intern look forward to the dreaded coffee runs."

His words did little to soothe the anger simmering inside me.

"At least tell me he can fix whatever he did," he begged.

Unless his sister suddenly vanishes off the face of the earth. I shook my head.

Sighing exasperatedly, Xander pushed, "Cat, seriously, the kid is crushed. Absolutely devastated."

"Not my problem," I replied callously, taking a small step forward as the line adjusted.

"I never want to be on your shit list."

"It's never a good place to be."

"Look at me," he said dramatically, sweeping a long arm up and down his fine muscular figure. "I'm a freaking architect doing a stupid coffee run."

"You could've had another intern do it."

"Except Ben and I kinda like David. He's got some serious potential to be a great architect. I mean, nowhere as fabulous as yours truly."

A small smile tugged at my lips.

"But we like him," Xander continued. "And we like you, which is why I'm doing a stupid coffee run. I wanted to check on you."

"That's sweet," I admitted, somewhat surprised two guys I just met kind of care about me. Or maybe I should be slightly concerned. *Hmmm.* "But I'm honestly fine."

The suspicious side eye he cast conveyed he didn't believe me.

"What are you doing tomorrow night?"

"Drinking my favorite wine in my pajamas while watching movies on the couch. I'm pretty sure ice cream will be involved too," I replied, without an ounce of shame my 23-year-old body wouldn't be hitting the bars over the weekend.

"Ben's brother owns a bar near the university," Xander explained. "Come out with us tomorrow night."

Falling asleep on my couch during a movie marathon and sleeping in late sounded so much better.

I shook my head. "Sorry. I really don't feel like going out."

"Please," he begged, slightly bouncing in place as if he was a toddler pleading with his mom for a piece of candy. "He won't be there. I swear on my boyfriend's mother's life."

The tall gorgeous architect made a cross sign over his heart with his index finger for added measure.

"Your boyfriend's mother's life, eh?" I grinned slightly.

"We could play darts all night long."

Aw, fuck. I puffed out my cheeks, slowly exhaling, as my mind perked up at the thought of playing a few rounds of darts. But then the logical part swiftly pointed out my love for the game led to the current frustratingly situation. *Drinking wine at home never hurt anyone.*

"I'm sorry, Cat," Xander said, noticing my hesitation, and shook his head. "You're giving me no choice but to use my last resort."

"Which is?" I arched an eyebrow with curiosity.

"Have Ben talk to you in Spanish. Low, sensual, slow."

My nether region cheered for joy, but I scowled at him. "You wouldn't dare."

With a shit-eating grin, he pulled his phone from his pants pocket and showed me a screen with Ben's number on it. "Try me, Cat," he taunted. "Just try me."

"Fine," I said, with resigned exasperation, as if I was the mom giving into the kid's demand for candy. "But, seriously, I'm out of there if I see him."

"Fair enough."

"I hate you both right now," I grumbled, sitting on a well-worn bar stool, as Xander pulled a long swig from his beer pint while perched on a stool next to me at the bar.

"Hey, how was I supposed to know that one dartboard wasn't working and a group of frat guys would hog the other one all night?" he protested, without a hint of remorse.

Named after Ben's niece's favorite ice cream, The Tin Roof was a hole-in-a-wall bar near one of the universities. It lured students with cheap beer, free popcorn, and loud music from a cash-accepted digital jukebox.

I looked amazingly cute too in a black cherry print skater dress paired with thick heeled black sandals, believing my feet needed some comfort from the expected standing and walking for hours. But my mood soured dramatically when the dumb college guys played game after game.

So, Xander and I drank and talked with Ben who ended up behind the counter when one of the bartenders called in sick. The night wasn't exactly a win, but I enjoyed getting to know Xander and Ben, another first-year architect.

"Niña bonita," Ben said, shaking his head at me and placing a fourth – or fifth – vodka tonic with lime in front of me.

"Thank you," I said, accepting the fresh drink. "But, unfortunately, you're pretty little words won't make me hate you any less."

"Mientras hablo lento y sensualmente, le haré débil," he practically whispered, leaning on his forearms on the counter and looking straight into my eyes. "Incluso con palabras simples como gato o manzanas."

If Ben's girlfriend didn't marry him, I had no problem proposing to him the nanosecond she broke his kind heart.

"Fine," I said, with a defeated sigh. "I don't hate you."

With a smug chuckle, he pushed himself off the counter when the door breezed open with a group of students walking in and laughing loudly.

Even before Ben frowned and muttered something in Spanish, I knew *he* was here.

A mix of irritation and curiosity made me wonder how the fuck my mind or even my body recognized his presence without a single fucking clue.

I quickly sucked down my drink through the tiny little straw; the coolness of the liquid doing nothing to alleviate my rising anger. After throwing a twenty dollar bill on the counter, I hopped off the stool and disappointingly wobbled the landing.

"Come on, Cat, I'll take you home," Xander said, throwing back the rest of his beer.

I held up my hand. "It's okay. I want to walk awhile, and then I'll catch a cab or something."

Rolling his eyes to the highest of heavens, he shook his head. "I'm not letting you walk by yourself at night. That's the dumbest idea I've ever heard."

Countering his dramatic eye roll, I rolled mine just as hard and shoved my thumb over my shoulder. "I won't be alone because I'm sure he'll follow me."

"Are you sure?" He grabbed both my hands and squeezed gently, and my heart filled with appreciation for my new friend. "I promised you he wouldn't come. So, say the word, Cat, and I'll tell Ben to kick him out."

I snickered at the thoughtful gesture.

"I'm sure," I replied, quickly pressing my lips to one of his ebony cheeks. "On the plus side, I get to yell and swear at him again."

Xander and David's heated and muffled voices carried outside as I greedily gulped the fresh night air. Summer nights were the best when the air was still warm but slightly cooler after the sun set.

Not even bothering to wait for David to creepily follow, I started walking down the well-lit block, full of rundown houses that served as off-campus housing. Rock music blared from open windows, indicating a good amount of students chose to stay in the area after the school year ended.

The party area expanded to the front steps and porches, filling the air with cigarette smoke, raunchy jokes and lewd comments, and the smell of spilled beer and cheap alcohol.

"I'm sorry, Cat." Frustration and tiredness laced through David's voice. "I am the biggest fucking moron. Ever."

Not gonna argue with you there, buddy.

Keeping my lips tightly pursed, I kept walking and ignored David's audible sighs as he followed closely. We probably looked like a normal college couple fighting since I counted three different couples acting the same way during my short trek.

"She's my best friend!" one girl shrieked from a front yard across the street. "How could you?"

"Cat," David said gruffly. "I'm sorry. I feel fucking terrible."

Well, you should feel fucking terrible. Idiot.

"Can we please talk?" he begged, his fingers brushing my arm and causing me to flinch from his warm and comforting touch.

With my mind completely disgusted at my body for wanting to give in, my mouth remained shut and my legs continued walking without a final destination.

With an agitated growl, David stepped in front of me with a locked jaw of determination and incredibly nervous green eyes.

Heat radiated through my body as my eyes narrowed in on his stupid denim jeans showcasing his long legs and a stupid gray t-shirt revealing his muscled arms. Even with desperation and misery written all over him, he still looked sexy as fuck.

Ugh. I absolutely hated how my body instinctively wanted to rip off his clothes and jump into his arms.

"I'm sorry, Cat," he choked out, running his fingers through his hair. "I should've trusted you."

Yup, you should have, you fucking dummy.

"Please talk to me. Say something, please."

"Go away, David," I snarled before stepping around him and continuing my brisk angry walk.

"She's gone," he shouted frantically, almost tempting me to stop and turn around.

Big whoop. She's gone. Except nothing can stop her from coming back.

"I told her I never wanted to see her again."

Before my mind could replay his words, my body halted so abruptly that David barely caught himself from crashing into me.

Choking back a moan from the brush of his body heat, I slowly faced him with a serious and doubtful look.

"I confronted her last night," he stammered as his hand reached for his dark blonde locks. "I asked her about everything you said, and, of course, she denied it all."

I rolled my eyes and moved to turn away again when he blurted out, "I know she lied. I saw something in her eyes that made realize she was lying."

What did he see?

"Cat, you were right from the start. She hasn't changed at all, and I'm a fucking dumbass for even believing she could change."

Why did my heart just soften a fraction? Because he should feel like a fucking dumbass, right?

"I changed my phone number so she can't even reach me. Even my mom promised not to give it to Gail although I highly doubt she'd reach out to Mom anyway."

Did his actions matter anyway? She was always going to be his sister. He had every right to choose her over me again and again.

My heart curled up in sadness at the realization as I sighed in resignation, feeling my rage and alcohol-fueled buzz subside.

"Cat," he said softly, hesitantly reaching for my hand. "I am so sorry I doubted you. I feel like a fucking idiot for hurting you."

The warmth of his thumb lightly drawing circles over my hand calmed my anger, but my doubts about us remained strong. So fucking strong.

I nodded slightly, not trusting my voice, as I gently pulled my hand away from his. As I started to walk away from him for the umpteenth time, I stopped suddenly and looked at him.

"What did you see?" I asked blankly.

"What?" His eyes blinked with confusion.

"You said you saw something in her eyes that made you realize she was lying."

David immediately looked down at the sidewalk, kicking a crushed plastic cup into someone's front yard, and rubbed the back of his neck.

As the silence stretched out, my irritation and impatience grew stronger.

"Amusement," he whispered so softly that I almost didn't hear him. "When I repeated your stories, she almost looked proud. Happy even."

Of course, my misery fucking amused her.
"I need a fucking drink," I grumbled bitterly, storming toward the closest party house.

Coffee and Chill

avid and I easily blended into the loud and crowded house party. Guys wearing cargo shorts, T-shirts, and baseball caps hollered and laughed. Girls wearing short shorts or ripped denim cutoffs and low-cut camisoles whispered and gossiped. Couples in corners played tonsil hockey and groped each other.

The house itself was a complete disaster area with sticky floors from spilled drinks, discarded clothes from any game that required stripping, and opened drawers and cabinets from anyone looking for more alcohol or drugs.

Good luck getting the full deposit back, I thought maturely, weaving through the thick mass of students.

"Cat," David yelled, sticking close behind me. "This isn't a good idea."

I ignored him and his toned frame that brushed against my back, wiggling my way into the kitchen. About four or five dozen guys dutifully guarded the kegs and at least two dozen half-empty bottles of hard alcohol.

Spying a half-empty bottle of flavored rum, I pressed a ten dollar bill into one of the guys' hand as I snatched the bottle off the counter.

"Thank you for your business," the guy shouted after me, and I lifted it in the air, showing my gratitude.

Subtle flavors of toffee and coconut immediately warmed the inside of my chest and pushed out any conflicting thoughts in my mind. A new wave of anger tore through me. I was fucking mad. I was mad at David. I was mad at Gail. I was mad at myself.

"She's your fucking sister, David," I shouted against the noise, holding the bottle of rum in my fist and stopping just outside the kitchen entrance. "What happens when she returns again?"

"Come on, Cat," he said loudly as people stumbled around us. "Let's get out of here and talk."

I shook my head, stomped my foot like a little child, and pulled a long swig of the liquid courage. "No, tell me now. What's gonna happen when you see her at Thanksgiving? Or Christmas?"

David sighed exasperatedly, gently tugging his hair with his fingers. "I haven't spent the holidays with her in years because she refuses to spend time with our mom."

"She's still your fucking sister," I repeated for lack of a better response.

"Just biologically. As of last night, I've decided I'm an only child raised by a single mother."

"What if she comes back? What if she really changed?"

David stepped closer, his hard chest brushing against mine and his warm breath tickling my ear. "None of that matters, Cat," he explained. "She could come back as a fucking nun for all I care because I choose you."

I choose you.

What did that even mean even though my poor heart careening at unsafe speeds had a pretty good idea.

"What?" I asked dumbfounded, narrowing my eyes at him and searching for any sign of amusement.

"I choose you," David repeated slowly and seriously as his stare never wavered.

"Why?" I demanded. "Why the fuck would you choose me over your own sister?"

Because even my own sister and mother deliberately chose to ignore my truth and believed his sister's words.

"Is it true, Catherine?" my mother had hissed, her green eyes flashing with rage. "Are you having sex with that boy?"

I forced myself to not roll my eyes since my parents found it highly disrespectful. "No, Mom. I didn't have sex with Marty Pullman."

"She's lying!" my older sister, Savannah, had whined, shoving an index finger in my face. "My friends saw her making out with him between classes."

I batted her perfectly manicured finger away, believing her friends were a bunch of idiots anyway. "I wasn't making out with him. Did your friends watch me knee him in the balls?"

"Then why is everyone saying you," she had argued before lowering her voice to a whisper, "that you know how to please a guy?"

"Because it's a rumor," I had replied through gritted teeth. "Like when you told your friends Lizzie had cancer last winter when the truth was she had the flu."

My older sister, who was a senior at the time, casually shrugged her shoulders at the memory of telling everyone our younger sister, Elizabeth, was dying from cancer for all the sympathetic attention.

"She could've had cancer. You don't know. You're not a doctor."

"Neither are you," I had shot back heatedly.

"Enough!" our mom had snapped, tilting her head slowly at each of us as if daring us to talk back to her. We never did. She had the power to stop an argument with one word and one menacing, cold stare.

"Catherine," she had said firmly. "Are you seeing a boy your father and I haven't met? You know that's against the rules."

I shook my head.

"Catherine," my mom had repeated, with a harder edge to your voice. "Don't lie to me."

"I'm not," I had answered truthfully, staring into her hard, angry eyes. "I don't have a boyfriend."

Even at age sixteen, I hadn't even experienced my first kiss unless Jake Harding's quick smooch, which was based on a dare by his stupid friends, in first grade counted. Between being an honor student, concentrating on my running, and working at the local grocery store, my free time had been pretty limited.

"She's lying!" Savannah had shrieked, with horror. "Everyone at school is talking about it. It's so embarrassing. Rumors start with some truth."

To my surprise, our mom nodded in agreement. "Rumors don't appear out of thin air, Catherine."

Did she seriously not know how vicious and unreasonable kids could be these days?

"You're grounded for a week, Catherine," my mom had declared as my dumbass older sister smiled triumphantly.

"Are you fucking kidding me?" I had cried out indignantly.

As soon as the words fell from my mouth, my mom's quick hand made unforgiving fierce contact with my tender cheek. Savannah's smile dropped immediately as her eyes went wide with fear. While our parents didn't believe in physical discipline, they knew how to make our lives miserable without it anyway.

"With a hideously filthy mouth like that, Catherine Cynthia Coleman," my mom had hissed, with so much venom in her voice. "No wonder everyone at your school thinks you're a slut."

One of my hands gingerly grazed the stinging cheek as my sister's eyes grew even wider at our mom's vicious tone and cruel words.

That night as I locked myself in my room and cried over my mom's inability to even trust me, I realized I couldn't even count on my family for any type of support. Absolutely none.

"Cat?" David asked, creasing his brows at me. "I choose you because you've never lied to me."

"You shouldn't," I muttered, gulping down another healthy shot of rum. "You don't even know me."

"I know enough. I know you would choose a lifetime supply of coffee over the finest wine. I know you cheered for every single teammate during a race, encouraging them to keep going. I know you prefer hardcover books over paperbacks."

Shit. He was right about my love for coffee and my book preference.

"And, I know you like me," he continued, biting his lower lip. "We both know there's something really good between us."

Fuck. He was right. I liked him more than I should. And we wouldn't be standing in the middle of a college keg party arguing if there wasn't something good between us.

"Don't you know I'm crazy about you?" David asked, slightly cocking his head to one side. "I've had a massive crush on you since like seventh grade."

"What?" I squeaked out; my tone soaring ten octaves higher.

He laughed before scrubbing a hand down his face. "I'm surprised you didn't know because my friends teased me all the fucking time."

I had no idea, but then again, I had been too busy with other priorities and responsibilities back then.

"You honestly didn't know?"

I shook my head causing some of my hair to fall in my face. David hesitantly reached out and brushed a few tendrils away from my eyes.

"I have liked you for so long, Cat," he admitted, his fingers gently caressing my warm cheek. "Just seeing you in the hallways at school made my day brighter. I worked hard to be a better runner to impress you. I wanted you to notice me."

With his palm resting lightly against my skin, my anger and resentment started to fade. I mentally cursed myself for letting go so easily. I wanted to hate him. I wanted to be mad at him.

"I promise to choose you every single time," he repeated, gently pressing his forehead against mine. "I promise."

Why? That simple one-word question popped into my mind again. Why would he choose me when we've never been on a date? Why was I even worthy to be chosen over someone else? Because I had never lied to him?

Given the chance would I lie to him? I wondered. Should I admit I couldn't get through the first

Harry Potter book? Should I tell him about my secret crush on Niall Horan?

You are enough, a tiny voice whispered in the back of my mind, catching me by surprise, but buried itself into my uncertain soul.

I closed my eyes and nuzzled into his hand still cupping my cheek. Even with the loud music pumping through the speakers and drunk students clumsily brushing past us, I somehow felt safe with David. Now that he knew the truth about Gail, I desperately wanted to trust him completely. But right now, I trusted him enough.

When I opened my eyes, he held my gaze and patiently waited for me to say or do something. Tilting my head ever so slightly, I pressed my lips against his and breathed in his heat. With both of his hands now holding my face as if to prevent me from running away, my tongue ran across his bottom lip before being welcomed by his.

I pressed my body against his as my hand still fisted the bottle of rum and held it against his hard chest. Before either of us could get lost in the kiss and each other, David pulled back breathlessly.

"Cat," he said huskily. "Let's get out of here."

I nodded and handed the bottle to the person closest to me before grabbing David's hand to lead us outside.

"Heeey," the drunk student slurred. "I'm not – oh, wait – thanks!"

Moving with the chaotic flow of the crowd led us into a brightly lit and sparsely populated hallway. About half a dozen students with plastic cups in their hands leaned against the walls and chatted quietly with each other.

A small door burst open, and a couple stumbled out, hastily adjusting their clothes. Without any thought or hesitation, I yanked on David's hand, pulling him into the small laundry room, and locked the door.

Easily catching me as I jumped into his arms and wrapped my legs around his waist, he set me on the edge of the dryer as his mouth ravaged mine.

Grinding my heated core against his erection, I moaned with so much damn desire.

"Cat," he growled frustratingly. "You're drunk. We can't – "

"Please," I begged, weaving my hands through his hair. "I want you so bad."

"I want you too, but this isn't how I imagined our first time together – "

I quickly pulled back from tugging on his earlobe between my teeth to study him with great curiosity.

"You thought about this?" I asked incredulously, briefly wondering if he thought about me when he rubbed one out.

A pink tinge slowly warmed his cheeks leading him to bury his face in the crook of my neck.

"Well, yeah," David murmured against my skin. "I think about you all the time."

Holy shit! My heart sang out with happiness. *He thinks about you. All. The. Time!*

"Was our first time going to be in your SUV in the parking ramp?" I teased, remembering how I loved his firm grip on my ass.

"Probably." He nuzzled my neck, causing me to giggle as his light scruff tickled me. "I couldn't control myself, seeing you in that cute red dress. Never wear pants to work."

I closed my eyes, feeling the heat of his hands on my hips. "You like my legs?"

"I fucking love your long sexy legs. I love imagining my head between them even more."

Holy fucking hell. I suppressed every single urge in my aroused body to shove his face below my waist because I desperately wanted to feel his mouth on me. The thought of being completely naked with him, feeling his warm skin against mine, made me shudder with pleasure.

"David," I whined, skimming my fingers under the hem of his t-shirt to lightly touch his chiseled abs. "Please."

"Fuck," he swore hoarsely. "You're not making this easy, are you?"

Damn his fucking conscience and gentleman ways!

With a sly and, hopefully, seductive smile, I hopped off the dryer and slowly pulled up the hem of my dress. Thanks to the beautiful mixture of vodka and rum in my system, I radiated confidence as my hands slowly slid my black lacy thong down my legs.

I bit my lower lip, watching his eyes darken with heat and lust and his body tighten with sexual energy. I held the delicate piece of material between my fingers before dropping it, but David easily caught it with one hand and quickly shoved it in the front pocket of his jeans.

As I raised an eyebrow with amused curiosity, he pressed me against an empty wall as his mouth slammed into mine again.

"Cat," he moaned as one of his hands dipped into the deep v-neckline of my dress.

I trembled in anticipation and sighed deeply when his fingers teased a taut nipple. Just as I lifted a leg to hook around his, David suddenly spun me around to face the wall. With my palms splayed against the plain white surface, I felt his hot breath against my neck and his fingers slowly inching up the front of my thighs.

When his hand fisted the hem of my dress and lifted it up, I groaned, feeling the warm air lightly dance across my sensitive and exposed area.

"Fuck," I whimpered.

With one strong hand splayed across my stomach over the fabric of my dress, the other hand slipped between my legs and grazed over my wet pussy.

"Shit," I cried out, resting my head against his shoulder.

"Do you like this?" David hummed playfully in my ear.

"Fuck yes."

When his thumb circled my clit with the perfect amount of pressure, I choked down a heated sob even though the high volume of the party probably would drown it out.

"Fuck," I yelled the second he slipped a finger inside me.

"Shit, Cat," he cursed, his lips brushing through my hair. "You're so fuckin' wet."

Even as I slammed my ass against his erection, his hand against my stomach held me tight as a second digit slid into me. The overwhelming intensity shot bright white stars into my vision.

"Are you going to come for me?" David whispered as his lips dusted my neck.

I nodded vigorously as his fingers deftly plunged in and out and his thumb expertly stroked my sweet bundle of nerves. As soon as I felt his teeth gently dig into my shoulder through the material of my dress, my release shattered into waves of euphoria.

"David," I moaned, succumbing to the millions of sensations shooting through my body. "David."

The kid was a fucking natural.

But his magical fingers ignored my words and the spasms of my body as a second crest of pleasure quickly formed and burst inside.

"David," I whined, resting my forehead against the wall, as a third –

"Hey!" a male voice shouted on the other side of the door followed by hard pounds. "Other people want to have sex now!"

My eyes flew open as the warmth of his hands fled with lightning speed from my body. The loud, hard knocks distracted me from the loss as my hands automatically straightened out my dress and my hair in case the guy barged through the flimsy door.

As I glanced in his direction, David adjusted himself with one hand as he seductively licked clean the two fingers – one by one – that had been inside me.

Holy shit. The ache between my legs cried out at the injustice of being robbed a third orgasm.

"Hurry the fuck up!" a female voiced yelled, spinning me back into reality.

Groaning with minor frustration at the lack of privacy and time, I buried my face in David's chest as he wrapped his arms around me. He chuckled and planted a kiss in my hair.

"It's not funny, David."

"It's kinda funny," he said, pulling back slightly and cupping my face to meet his serious gaze. "I promise there won't be any interruptions next time, Cat."

Next time. My heart melted on the spot next to a pile of dirty clothes.

The moment David unlocked and opened the door, the next couple frantically rushed in and practically pushed us out of the small room with the slam of the door.

Feeling my cheeks warm with a hint of shyness and embarrassment, he quickly pulled me flush against him.

"You're amazing," he murmured, leaning his forehead against mine.

"Amazing enough to get my panties back?" I asked, suddenly conscious of the warm night air slipping between my legs.

With a wicked smile spreading across his face, he shook his head and whispered in my ear. "Not a chance. And, by the way, next time I want to hear you scream my name when I make you come."

Holy fucking shit, I thought breathlessly as my core pulsated with excited anticipation. *This man was going to kill me with sex.*

Considering what just happened in the laundry room, I was perfectly fine with death by orgasm.

David grinned lazily, lacing his fingers through mine, and led us back to the party.

"Baby, your phone is ringing!"

A wide smile crossed my face as I threw on my favorite pair of navy cotton shorts and a white t-shirt with navy print. I loved hearing him use the simple term of endearment.

Four beautiful sex-filled and disgustingly delirious weeks have passed since David chose me over his soul-sucking sister. And he kept his promise to make me scream his name in bed – repeatedly.

Maybe we needed to go through all the drama to reach this stage of happiness and contentment. Our relationship was far from perfect, especially after learning he disliked sushi and movies with subtitles. David mocked me for days when I admitted I had never seen the movies *The Usual*

Suspects or *Fight Club*. We had spent a weekend watching our favorite movies, and I loved everything about *The Usual Suspects*. *Fight Club* not so much since I figured out the twist somewhere near the middle of the movie.

We spent most of our time in my one-bedroom apartment since my floor wasn't littered with loose change and junk mail and I didn't live with two other guys named Jamie and Aaron. Although David preferred spending the night at my place, he missed the comfort of his California King bed, which gave him room to stretch out and roll around without disturbing me. My dinky full-size bed was a bit snug, but we made it work.

The thought about buying a bigger bed or even suggesting David move his crossed my mind a few times, but I wasn't quite ready for that conversation. I was completely content getting to know him and hanging out with our friends or at home. And, of course, I loved rolling around in either bed – or car for that matter – with him until we were both completely exhausted and satisfied.

Except I nervously waited for someone – me, him, Gail, anyone really – to deflate our bubble of happiness. What would happen if David asked me to give up coffee? Could I give up my favorite my beverage in the whole entire world for him? And what kind of monster would ask that of me? Basically, what would happen if David and I reached an impasse on an important matter? Unanswered questions bothered me.

"Answer your fucking phone!" David yelled from the living room as I dumped my clothes in a hamper.

What the fuck? I frowned, knitting my eyebrows in confusion. I should probably give him a chance to explain his outburst before I unleashed hell upon his soul.

"That's what Lizzie's text said!"

Ah, that makes more much sense. A huge sigh of relief washed over me as I left my room and joined my ridiculously gorgeous boyfriend on my dark gray couch. He appeared relaxed and settled, playing around on his phone on one end of the couch, with the recliner stretched out to rest his legs. We returned a few moments ago after stuffing ourselves at my favorite Chinese restaurant with Xander and Ben.

Grabbing my phone laying on the middle seat, I snuggled into David's side as I scanned messages from my younger sister, Lizzie.

"Fuck off," I muttered, with an exasperated sigh.

"What's going on?" David asked, brushing his soft lips over my forehead.

"My sister, Lizzie, wants to buy this super expensive computer for our grandmother for her 85th birthday. She says it will be super easy for Mims to learn."

"Let me guess. Your grandma is against technology."

Resting my head against his shoulder, I shrugged slightly as I sent a quick message to my sister, politely saying Mims wouldn't want a computer. "Kind of? She loves the tablet I bought for her for reading and playing games. But that's all she does with it – reads and plays games."

Due to my strained relationship with my family, I desperately wanted to flee to some exotic location after graduating from high school. But my conscience refused to let me stray too far from my beloved Mims, my paternal grandmother who resided in an assisted living facility. We bonded over our shared love for books when she caught me reading a smutty novel in her library during a family gathering. I had been eleven at the time and didn't quite understand why a man wanted to kiss the area where a woman went to the bathroom.

Not only did Mims allow me to finish, she handed me a more appropriate book and instructed me to quickly switch in case my parents or any other adult checked on me. She threw me a sly wink before returning to the party, and I believed I had the coolest grandma ever.

So when she couldn't read her beloved paperbacks due to poor eyesight, I bought a simple tablet for her, set everything up, and showed her how to use it during a visit. She objected at first because she loved "flipping through the pages," but she relented when she realized no mouse was involved and everything was ready at her fingertip. She fell deeper in love when I showed her all the card games she could play against the computer.

"Mims is a little old fashioned," I said thoughtfully, waiting to hear what my sister thought about my comment. "She still sends birthday cards through the mail and prefers to talk to someone face to face. I'm not sure if she would like talking to a computer screen."

"Is the rest of your family on board with the gift?" David asked, intertwining our hands to kiss my knuckles.

"According to Lizzie, everyone is on board except for me."

"So do you have to go home for her birthday?"

I closed my eyes and groaned at the mere thought of returning to our Minnesota hometown. He chuckled, accepting my disgruntled noise as a yes.

"Mims is the only reason I go back for the holidays," I admitted, opening my eyes and studying our interlocked hands resting on his thigh. "I even stay with her in her tiny two-bedroom apartment at the facility."

"You don't stay with your parents? I thought you were close with your family."

I snorted and shook my head. "Fuck no. My parents pretty much disowned me when I refused to study medicine. I didn't even have to be a doctor or anything – although that would've made them incredibly happy – I could've been a researcher or something. It just had to be in the medical field."

"Didn't like the sound of Dr. Coleman?" he asked playfully.

Shaking my head again, I said, "For as long as I could remember, I loved colors and patterns. I wanted to be an artist for awhile because I loved sketching and painting, but I lacked passion. I dunno, but something about designing a room just clicked with me."

"Your parents seriously didn't support you finding your own path?" Genuine surprise registered in his voice as he turned to rest on his side to face me.

My parents, I thought to myself, closing my eyes and picturing my parents. My dad, with strong handsome Asian features, stood a little over six feet and kept a fit frame by bicycling every day. In comparison, my mom reminded me of a porcelain doll with her fair complexion and shoulder length strawberry blonde hair.

Part of me stayed somewhat close to home – if seven to eight hours was considered close – secretly hoping they would realize they were being asshats and would accept me back into the family with open arms and tearful apologies.

Leaning my head against the cushioned couch with my legs tucked underneath, I shrugged because I had accepted their disapproval long before graduating high school. "They'd be embarrassed if I redesigned the interior of an art museum or concert hall. When I stood my ground that I wanted to pursue this career, they said they wouldn't support me."

"I'm so sorry, Cat," David said softly, tapping my nose and making me smile. "That really sucks."

"Why did you think I was close with my family?"

"Lizzie. Even though she's a year younger than me, we had the same circle of friends in high school. She talked about you all the time. Never said anything bad."

He snickered as I scrunched my nose and wrinkled my eyebrows in complete confusion and doubt. "I'm pretty sure you were talking to a different Lizzie. I mean Elizabeth is a popular name."

My sisters and I were close until Savannah secretly kissed Max Williams at a friend's birthday party in fifth grade. Believing Max was her one true love, she immediately started planning their future the moment she returned home. I believed she was stupid crazy when she created dozens of Pinterest boards dedicated to her life with Max. Savannah immediately called me an idiot, saying a third-grader didn't know "anything about true love."

With a three-year age gap, Lizzie and I didn't have anything in common. My nose was always stuck in a book or my hands were doodling something in one of my many sketchbooks. She usually ran around the neighborhood with her cluster of friends. Our relationship changed dramatically when she called me "selfish bitch" for not pursuing a medical career and I tossed back she was a spoiled, entitled demon child desperately craving our parents' approval.

"What exactly did she say?" I asked, refusing to believe my younger sister even had the ability to say something nice about me.

Shrugging slightly, David said, "I dunno. Just basic stuff like you joined the cross country team in college, and you were having a good time."

Oh, she's good. She's not exactly lying when being vague, I thought, wondering how she knew I was on the cross country team. Lucky guess? I deleted all my social media accounts when I moved because my family didn't even deserve to stalk me on the web.

"I didn't know you guys hung out in high school," I said, feeling a slight twinge of jealousy shoot through me.

"Some of her friends were dating some of my friends," he explained nonchalantly. "I only saw her when our friends were together."

Chewing on my lower lip to keep myself from asking more stupid questions, I wondered why I didn't talk to him all that much during the cross country seasons. The boys and girls teams were small enough that everyone knew each other but also big enough to separate the junior varsity from the varsity members.

"Hey," David said softly, nudging my nose with his. "You a little jealous?"

I quickly buried my face into the back cushion to hide my suddenly pink cheeks and stupid scowl as he chuckled lowly, running his fingers over my bare knees.

"Answer me," he demanded teasingly as his hands slid under my knees.

I silently shook my head, completely mortified to be envious of my sister.

"Cat." His light warning growl made me smile at his playfulness as my blush deepened.

Without warning, David's strong hands gripped the back of my knees and pulled my legs toward his lap. Yelping with surprise and flailing around like a fish caught on a hook, I felt the seat cushions against my back as David slowly and seductively climbed over me with a silly grin.

"Cat." Same light growl lit a fire between my legs.

I caught his green eyes darken with need before twisting my neck to face the back cushion. I was still too fucking embarrassed to look at him.

"Don't be jealous," he said as he feathered soft kisses over my neck. "You were the only reason why I even talked to her. She wasn't even my type."

The reason for my bashfulness suddenly swerved from Lizzie's time with him to David's sincere words. Every damn day spent with him, I was showered with different kinds of kisses, small touches, sweet or naughty texts, and some seriously thoughtful gestures. I had never felt so special – or loved – in my life.

With just one look, he possessed the power to make my heart plunge into my belly and then rocket back into my chest, making me completely breathless.

"Besides, there has always been only one Coleman girl for me," David whispered in my ear, nibbling on my lobe and causing the fire between to spread and burn hotter.

Plastering on my most coying smile, I turned my head to look at him with wide innocent eyes. "Is it me?" I whispered breathlessly.

"Damn fucking right," he muttered before devouring my mouth possessively.

Sighs of pleasure slipped from my throat as his tongue smoothly glided against mine and my hips arched to meet his. Just as my fingers opened a button his light blue dress shirt, David pulled back and gazed at me hesitantly.

"I love you, Cat," he said, his voice heavy with emotion, as a dash of fear and honesty flickered in his green eyes. "I think I've loved you since seventh grade."

I smiled shyly as my heart soared with pure happiness.

How could I not love this man who slides a protective arm around my waist or over my shoulder when walking through a huge crowd of people? The man who learned I hate tomatoes on my sandwiches but love them in salads. The man who watched my favorite movie, *Sense and Sensibility*, without a single complaint or snide comment. The man who promised to protect me from his soulless sister.

"I love you too," I replied softly.

David grinned brightly before crashing his mouth onto mine again and weaving his hands into my hair. My fingers skimmed down his sides and tugged at his shirt, pulling it free from his pants.

I could easily spend hours trailing my fingers over his magnificently sculpted and naked body, mesmerized by each indentation, freckle, and scar. I loved how his body covered mine. As if he was protecting me. As if he was submitting himself to only me.

I inhaled sharply and instinctively curved my body into his when his hand slipped underneath my t-shirt and ran it over a pebbled nipple.

"You're not wearing a bra!" David gasped, feigning shock, as his fingers continued to make my highly sensitive body part rock hard.

"Shit," I cursed, sliding a hand down my stomach to soothe my aching core.

Clicking his tongue against the roof of his mouth, he shook his head and grabbed my hand.

"Baby," I whined, bucking my hips up in search of some sort of friction. "Please."

Just as he wickedly smirked at me, his phone buzzed.

"Ignore it," David muttered, holding my dominant arm above my head, but his phone continued to buzz.

"Check it," I urged, relaxing my horny body. "It might be your mom."

Sitting up and grabbing his phone that had dropped to the floor, David scrunched his face with disapproval and frowned.

"What is it?" I sat up, pulling my t-shirt down.

"It's Annalise."

As in Annalise, his ex-girlfriend? *Stay cool, Cat, stay cool,* I reminded myself as I sucked in a deep breath.

"What does she want?" I really hoped I sounded casual and breezy and not jealous and suspicious.

"She wants to meet with me. She's in the area for some reason."

"She wants to see you now?"

"Yeah, she's really upset about something."

I silently picked imaginary lint from my shorts, not knowing how to respond. Being an over-controlling and clingy girlfriend was definitely not my nature, but how much control did his ex-girlfriend have over my boyfriend?

"Hey," David said softly, laying the phone on armrest and pulling me into his lap. "She has no reason to call me unless it's an emergency."

"What's wrong?" I had the right to ask that, right?

He shrugged as his hands slipped around my waist. "She wouldn't tell me, but I'm gonna call her and find out what's going on, okay?"

"If she's in the area, you should meet with her." My mind congratulated my voice for sounding responsible and rational. "You said she only calls when it's an emergency."

"But I wanna stay with you. I really need to see you naked."

I laughed, feeling his hands slip under my shirt and roam my back, as I tried to wiggle off his lap.

"Baby," he said huskily, planting kisses on my neck, as his hands dipped into the waistband of my shorts.

My resolve to be a responsible and mature adult started to fade as his fingers danced lightly across my ass and his erection pressed into my side.

"Fuck," I cursed, reluctantly pushing myself off his lap and onto the middle seat.

David sighed with frustration, scrubbing a hand down his face, and scrambled off the couch. "Being an adult is hard," he grumbled.

"It sucks, doesn't it?"

"Something else I'd rather suck." He threw me a naughty wink, and I scowled and crossed my legs in frustration.

Fuck. The thought of his tongue working magical wonders on my most intimate part had my mind and body sexually distracted. Being somewhat productive was out of the question until I found some sort of release –

"Hey," David said sharply, pointing two fingers at his eyes and then at mine. "No using your vibrator when I'm gone."

My mouth fell wide open in shock before curling into a full-on pout.

Raising a skeptical eyebrow, his facial expression read, *Yeah, go ahead and deny you weren't thinking about using your vibrator as soon as I left.*

"Promise me, Cat," he growled, narrowing his eyes at me. He stood in front of me, leaning over to grip the back of the couch with both hands and caging me in. "Promise me that you won't use your vibrator, your fingers, or any other sex toy while I'm gone."

Dammit! Telling him to meet his ex-girlfriend before satisfying my sexual needs was a fucking terrible idea. I really needed to work on being more selfish because danger, power, dominance, and any other word to describe control radiated from him. The way his eyes firmly held my stare. The way his body remained tight and sharp. The unspoken promise of punishment if I didn't obey him. The promise of complete satisfaction if I did.

Fuck! My fingers itched to rip open his dress shirt and just ravage him on the living room floor.

Sucking in a deep breath, I gritted out, "I promise."

Ducking his head a bit, David softly kissed my lips. "Or the shower massager."

Ah fuck, I was really screwed now.

"You're the worst," I shouted, scrunching up my face to hide my infuriating smile.

Grinning smugly and quickly kissing me once more, he stood up and headed toward my room. "I know."

"Fuck." With an irritated groan, I hauled my ass off the couch and poured myself a glass of wine. Flipping open my laptop on the kitchen counter, I parked my tush on a cushioned wooden stool and studied the screen.

My bubble of happiness included my job, still pulling double duty as Paige's personal assistant and what felt like administrative assistant to the office. Even though she rarely praised anyone for an outstanding job, I felt she liked me as her assistant since she hardly ever yelled at me. She yelled *for* me to do a whole bunch of stuff, but she hasn't driven me to tears – yet.

When one of the designers repeatedly failed to impress a client with a neutral-themed nursery, Paige opened the project to other designers and Summer strongly suggested I submit a portfolio. Jumping at the chance to showcase my talent and ideas, I focused on my design whenever I had a chance over the past few days. The proposal would definitely distract me from thinking too much about David and Annalise.

"Working on the Henderson project?" David asked, emerging from the room wearing khaki cargo shorts and gray t-shirt with the college logo printed across the chest.

I nodded, sipping my wine, as I felt his lips brush the back of my head.

"I don't know how long I'll be, but I'll message you when I'm headed back, okay?"

"You're a good guy," I said suddenly, realizing my luck. "I'm not close with any of my exes to call them in case of an emergency."

"Well, you have me now so you don't need to call them. Ever."

The small trace of jealousy in his voice made my heart swell as I hid my tiny smile behind the wine glass.

"Remember no touching!" he threw back teasingly before heading out the door.

"You're the worst," I called out and greedily gulped down the rest of my wine.

A Latte to Handle

"Hello, beautiful," David greeted, kissing me on the cheek before setting his lunch tray down on the table.

"Hey," I muttered; my eyes glued to the screen of my laptop as my fingers raced over the keyboard.

"What are you working on?"

"My portfolio for the Henderson project." I sipped my caramel iced coffee and sighed happily as the cool liquid soothed my frantic mind.

Just before I fell asleep last night a more brilliant idea for the neutral-themed nursery leaped into my mind with a soft gray and brown color scheme, framed photos of cute safari animals, and a giant plush giraffe toy. Unfortunately, I needed to complete my new portfolio as soon as possible to meet the end-of-the-day deadline as I scrapped my previous and unfinished concept. Fortunately, strokes of genius flowed through me at a rapid pace, and I felt confident with my work.

"I thought you finished that last night," David said, popping a kettle chip into his mouth.

I shook my head, keeping my eyes on the screen. "It wasn't even close to being finished, but a new idea hit me right before bedtime."

An almost inaudible "oh" escaped from his lips, and my head immediately snapped up to stare at him shifting uncomfortably in his seat and chewing on his lower lip.

"Your portfolio looked complete," David stammered, bowing his head and dropping his shoulders in defeat. "I thought it looked great."

I sharply sucked in a wad of fresh air and closed my eyes, deeply frightened to hear the next words.

"I submitted your portfolio before we went to bed last night. You're a perfectionist, Cat, and I thought you were too nervous to submit it. The cover letter was completed, and I simply attached the portfolio and sent it."

Damn my habit to complete the simple tasks first before tackling the tougher ones, I thought miserably as I snapped my laptop shut a little harder than I wanted. Propping my elbows on the table, my fingers rubbed my temples to alleviate the oncoming headache and, hopefully, to turn back time.

"Cat, I'm so sorry. I'll go and talk to your boss right now. I'll explain everything."

"No!" I stared at him, holding out my hands in a stop position. My reply sounded harsher and louder than I expected, especially when David appeared visibly crushed and remorseful for his "helpful" gesture. "I'm sorry. Please don't talk to Paige."

"But I'll tell her that it was my fault. She'll understand."

I grabbed his hand, foolishly believing I had the strength to keep my Adonis of a boyfriend from running up to the fifth floor and bursting into my boss' office. "I appreciate the thought, David. I really do, but you don't know her. She hates excuses. If anything, you would make the situation worse."

Signs of doubt crossed his handsome clean cut face.

Exhaling a soft breath and relaxing my face, I said gently, "Thank you for watching out for me, but promise me, you won't talk to my boss."

"I promise," he agreed reluctantly.

If David could promise his ex-girlfriend to temporarily keep her secret from me, then he should have no problem keeping his word to me.

I had been a bit miffed when he wouldn't share his conversation with Annalise from a few nights ago. Even the promise of a little butt play didn't tempt him to spill the beans. He reassured me he would tell me everything when he could. I didn't love the idea of him keeping something from me, but I also trusted him.

I trusted he wouldn't break his word because Paige would snap David in half with just one cold, hard look. She hated excuses, but she despised dramatic stories even more. She could care less that my boyfriend accidentally submitted my incomplete portfolio. All my boss wanted was results that met her high and demanding expectations.

However, I was somewhat bothered David believed his help was needed when it came to my work. Did he really assume my confidence was so low that I wouldn't submit anything out of fear of rejection or imperfection? While "chance" wasn't exactly my middle name, I still took them, knowing I wouldn't get far if I didn't.

What terrorized me the most was I couldn't think of a single good reason to explain my concept being a complete clusterfuck. The obvious "I sent it by mistake" argument sounded lame considering I wrote a polished and professional cover letter. Maybe Paige would understand a better idea hit me after my first submission, but would she see my plausible explanation as an excuse?

I had no doubt she would shred my incomplete portfolio and what little confidence I had to pieces, probably leaving me brokenhearted and devastated. Feelings of sadness and helplessness overwhelmed me as I blew my once chance to make a good impression.

David's constant parade of concerning messages after lunch did nothing to calm my nerves as I spent the rest of the day dreading to hear Paige call me into her office. Because I was a complete chicken shit to tell him face to face, I shot him a text saying I needed "me time" for the rest of the day. The thought of him watching me break down and turn into a hot mess filled me with more anxiety.

He certainly didn't need to witness me eat my feelings with a large bacon and mushroom pizza and drown my sorrow with my favorite bottle of wine. That magnificent shitstorm should be saved for special occasions liked being excluded from a family reunion or one of my sisters' weddings. Our relationship was still brand new, and I wanted to keep what little pride I had left.

Despite his numerous objections and "I want to be there for you" sentiments, David mentioned Xander and Ben were dragging him to a bar after work. I made a mental note to buy a few rounds the next time we hit a bar.

Even a tall caramel blended coffee drink with extra whipped cream drizzled with more caramel couldn't calm my nerves or remove the elephant-sized weight in my chest. My uncooperative brain still refused to find one good reason for submitting a shit design.

Fuck my life.

As the day slowly crawled toward the end, a teeny tiny piece of hope bloomed inside me. Maybe my incomplete portfolio wasn't even worth her valuable breath and time.

With five minutes left on the clock and my heart racing as if I had run an entire marathon in a full-on sprint, my body refused to relax until it was time to dodge out the fucking door.

"Cathy!" Paige yelled from her office.

So fucking close, I thought nervously. At least she doesn't sound angry.

Taking a deep breath, I entered her spacious and immaculate office decorated with modern and bold touches. A huge built-in wooden book case filled with hundreds of books covered the wall behind her desk.

My boss leaned back in her swivel chair, looking completely professional and emotionless.

"Sit." I automatically sat in the closest chair in my vicinity like a well-trained puppy eager to please.

We stared at each other for what seemed like an hour as I discreetly wiped my sweaty palms on my skirt and she methodically tapped the end of an pen against her clear glass desk.

She silently tossed a black leather portfolio in my direction on her desk. Chewing on my lower lip, I was surprised she wasted her precious time to assemble my incomplete design into a fancy binder. But then again I wouldn't be surprised if the file was actually empty or contained someone else's compositions.

Either way, I didn't reach for it to find out.

"Did you submit this?" Paige asked coolly, laying down her pen and steepling her fingers.

"Yes," I replied flatly, not even taking a chance to explain. Her question required one of two answers: yes or no. If she wanted a more in-depth answer, she would've asked why I submitted it.

"Are you proud of your work?"

"No," I answered honesty, holding her imposing stare.

She raised an eyebrow with interest, but I remained silent, hoping she'd give me a chance to explain.

"Do you really want to be an interior designer?"

"Yes," I said determinedly.

Paige pulled her chair forward and rested her arms on the clear surface. "I'll be honest with you, Cathy. I thought you had potential, but one look at your portfolio tells me you shouldn't even be in this field."

Fuck my life, I thought dejectedly, swallowing the huge lump in my throat and feeling my heart shatter into a million pieces. *Do not fucking cry.*

"Do you believe you belong here?"

"Yes," I replied in a surprisingly calm and clear tone.

Paige glanced at her phone before silently studying me for a more seconds. "You may go now."

My job was safe for now, I thought with a little bit of relief, leaving her office and grabbing my purse from my desk.

On the edge of breaking down, I ducked into the women's public restroom, locking myself in a stall, and rested my forehead against the cool and, hopefully, sanitized metal door. With tears streaming down my face, I desperately gasped for small breaths to prevent a full blown ugly cry.

"You shouldn't even be in this field."

I worked so fucking hard so I would never have to hear those devastating words. Everything I had accomplished to get here now meant nothing.

"Buck up, buttercup," Summer said breezily, throwing herself on my desk and picking up a letter opener.

Giving her a small smile, I continued to sort through a huge pile of unopened mail.

After a restless night of tossing and turning, I was grateful to still have a job this morning and more grateful Paige was out of the office for a morning meeting. My second cup of coffee did nothing to improve my discourage mood, and it wasn't even ten yet.

"*You shouldn't even be in this field.*" My mind seriously couldn't stop replaying her words.

Should I follow her advice – was that even advice to begin with – and give up on my dream? I didn't have a backup plan. Was I an idiot for putting all my eggs in one basket? Was coaching a cross country team hard? Was there money in coaching? Should I become an administrative assistant or personal assistant?

"So you had a minor setback, sweetheart," Summer continued, ignoring my silence and wielding the letter opener like a sword. "Another opportunity will come along. Our designers aren't the brightest, you know."

"Hey," Leslie, a long-time designer, protested indignantly as she walked by my desk carrying a load of sample books in her arms. "I heard that."

"You're the exception, Les," she called after her, winking at me. "Be patience, buttercup. She sees your worth."

Knitting my brows together, I shot her a questionable look.

"Athens wasn't built in a day, ya know."

"Rome," I corrected, holding out my hand for the letter opener. "Rome wasn't built in a day."

Summer frowned and placed the office tool in my hand. "But the Romans built Athens, right?"

"What?" History had never been my favorite class or my strongest subject, but I strongly suspected Athens was nowhere near Rome. Geography also wasn't one of my strongest subjects.

"My point being," she said, waving her hand dismissively. "You're smart and young, and you have the rest of your life to be an interior designer, Cat."

"Maybe," I muttered, neatly opening an envelope.

"Do you think my dream was to be an accountant slash human resource director at my best friend's company in the middle of a fucking cornfield?"

"What was your dream?"

"To marry Christian Slater and make dozens of gorgeous babies with him."

I puffed out my cheeks and exhaled an amusing breath.

"My point is when the shit hits the fan, you look for ways to either cover yourself or turn off the fucking fan."

"You should be a motivational speaker," I teased, with a genuine smile. "Turn your little life quotes into a book."

"See?" Summer said brightly, hopping off my desk and checking her phone for the time. "You're learning already. FYI, Paige will be back soon from her meeting with some city officials. Those meetings never go well."

Catching her drift, I grabbed my wristlet and headed down to the café. My favorite barista, Kacey, leaned against a back counter, looking bored, as she fiddled on her phone. Her sweet face immediately brightened as soon as I walked in.

"Give me something to do," she begged jokingly. "Keep me busy."

Laughing at her plea, I ordered a tall French roast for Paige and two tall chocolate mint mochas for me and Summer. Kacey and I leisurely chatted as she worked on my order.

"Thanks, Kace," I called out over my shoulder, feeling my spirits lift a bit. "You're the best."

"Tell me something I didn't know!" she tossed back good-naturedly.

My smile immediately vanished at the sight of a sneering blonde bitch standing outside the café's entrance.

"Here, kitty kitty," Gail mocked, with evil glee in her icy blue eyes, as I cautiously approached her.

Every fiber in my body wanted to throw the coffee order at her, ruining her skinny jeans, sheer white tank top, and multi-colored infinity scarf, and run for the hills. But I still had a bit of dignity left, and I didn't want to waste perfectly good coffee on a piece of shit.

"What the fuck do you want?" I asked bitterly, desperately praying this showdown wouldn't turn into an embarrassingly public shouting match.

"To break your pathetic heart, sweetheart," she said, in a sickening sweet tone. "You know it's only a matter of time before my brother dumps you and returns to his ex-girlfriend."

Surprisingly, I bit into my lower lip not to keep myself from becoming an emotional hot mess but to prevent myself from smirking at her blatant lies. She knew absolutely nothing about her amazing and kind brother and even less about our relationship.

"You will never be good enough for him," Gail continued, tucking a loose blonde tendril that escaped her perfectly casual ponytail. "Even your own family can't fucking stand you. If you're not even good enough for them, do you really believe you're good enough for anyone? I mean aren't parents supposed to unconditionally love their children?"

She's right, my own mind sang out viciously, shredding the last bits of my confidence. *You're not smart enough to even be an interior designer. Even your idiot younger sister got into a medical school, and what are you doing? Fetching coffee for other people.*

"I ran into Elizabeth a few days ago back home, and she and I talked for hours about how you're disappointing everyone in your pathetic little life. Did you know that when your parents meet new people they claim to have two daughters?"

Her brutal words easily shredded the last bit of hope I held for my parents actually being proud of me and my accomplishments. Did I really need to study medicine in order for my parents to love me? Was chasing a different dream so bad to be kicked out of a family?

"No one will ever remember you, kitty," Gail taunted, with a malicious and hateful smile. "No one."

"I'd rather be forgotten than be remembered for being a lying, soulless bitch that manipulated and purposely hurt people to get what she wanted," I spat out, with an equal amount of venom in my tone, as my eyes narrowed on hers. "I would never want to be remembered as being a selfish little twat."

I shoulder checked her hard as I stormed off with my head held high. I might have thrown in the last word – a pretty good dig and I would no doubt think of a better one in the days to follow – but my soul had been crushed.

Being remembered or leaving a legacy wasn't even a concern. Her incredibly lame attempt to sabotage my relationship with David didn't even faze me. No, the realization my own family – with the exception of Mims – gave up on me simply shattered me. Gail was right: weren't parents supposed to unconditionally love their children?

The chaos in my mind distracted me from noticing Paige following me to the elevator until she coolly stepped inside and punched the button to the fifth floor.

Keep it together, Cat, I thought nervously as I died a little bit inside. *Don't cry in front of your fucking boss.* Did she hear the whole conversation? Could I be fired for calling my nemesis a "twat"? Was Gail really my nemesis or more of a bully? Should I say something?

"Are you sick?" Paige demanded, carefully taking the coffee holder from my clammy hands.

I wanted to believe she cared about my well being, but I sensed she cared more about the full cups of coffee she now held.

Not trusting my own damn voice, I shook my head.

"You don't look well."

"I'm fine," I managed to squeak out, staring at the floor, as the elevator began its short ascent.

"You sound sick."

I snuck small quiet and deep breaths to help control my racing heart and my frantic emotions. When the elevator doors opened, my boss raced out first and headed straight to the office.

"Cathy, you're sick," she called over her shoulder to me. "Go home."

I headed toward my desk, wondering how to snag my beautiful mocha from her. "I'm fine, Ms. Ward."

"It's not a request. Go home before you infect the entire office."

My shoulders slumped in defeat at her demanding tone. "Yes, ma'am," I murmured quietly as a wave of emptiness and darkness crashed into my heart.

Everything I had worked so hard for meant nothing now.

I desperately hoped no one would remember me and my epic failures.

10

Caffeinate and Conquer

PAIGE

Tapping my fingers very slowly was a telltale sign I was pissed off beyond reason and no one – maybe except my father and Summer – should dare talk to me. Not one single word. If my fingers are tapping methodically on any surface, run far and fast.

The way the blonde waif sneered and taunted my assistant made my blood boil every time the scene replayed in my busy mind. No one messed with me and my company.

I immediately recognized the signature mean girl traits. Confident. Domineering. Arrogant. Natural beauty. She had the potential to become someone important, but instead, she used her strengths to mask her own vulnerabilities and weaknesses. She didn't use them to her advantage.

What a fuckin' cliché, I thought disgustingly.

The past fifteen years of my life was spent using my cold and calculated attributes to not only make my business successful but build a solid foundation and established reputation. I might have occasionally batted my long and sexy eyelashes, but my relentless drive and razor-sharp attitude made me an equal among my male colleagues.

I didn't care people called me a fierce or unforgiving bitch behind my back. I was proud to be a hard bitch who delivered demands and ultimatums. I thrived on tears and threats from my subordinates.

My employees' personal lives didn't interest me at all. I had no desire to know who was trying to have a baby, who was going through a divorce, or who was overcoming their haunted past.

I wanted competent, driven people that could turn off the fan when the shit hit it. I wanted people to work hard without complaint and strive and fight for the best.

As long as I had Summer, I didn't want or need a circle of friends. She was everything I wasn't – friendly, laid back, and personable – and she lived for all that personal shit. And, God bless her adorable little heart, she only told me what I needed to know if it affected my business.

Cat – yes, of course, I knew her name – was part of my badass team. Even adorned in her fashionably brightly colored skirts and dresses, she was a sharp and quick-thinking badass.

She might have gotten in the brutally honest last words after the supposedly humiliating encounter, but Cat still looked like she witnessed a kitten being run over by a semi-truck. Watching her struggle so fucking hard to keep her emotions in check sparked an unfamiliar feeling in the pit of my stomach. Compassion.

I sent her home for the day because if she stayed a minute longer I probably would've said "good job" or – even worse – smiled at her. Ranting at her about looking like shit and being highly contagious wasn't necessary, but hey, what the fuck did I know about compassion? Summer probably would've hugged her tightly, planned a murder in great detail, and then invited her for a girls' night out.

Cat's commitment and unrelenting hard work as an unpaid intern last year had surprised the fuck out of me. The other three entitled morons might have clocked in on time in the morning, but Cat was always the first to arrive. While they were always the first to leave at the end of the day, she was the first to volunteer to stay late.

The other interns had irritated the fuck out of me, constantly complaining to Summer about the lack of respect and responsibilities or bickering who would complete the more impressive or glamorous assignments. They had wanted glory and praise for doing absolutely nothing. Cat had been the only dependable one – in the past three years if I was being completely honest – which was why I offered her a full-time position.

Unfortunately, my fourth personal assistant this year proved to be incompetent, and I desperately needed help – which I only admitted to Summer, of course – and didn't have the time or patience to babysit someone new. So I reluctantly tapped Cat for the job until I found someone capable of stringing together a sentence without bursting into tears.

If she didn't have her heart set on becoming an interior designer, I would permanently keep her as my assistant because she exceeded my high expectations. I couldn't – no, wouldn't – lose Cat; I had big plans for her even though her Henderson portfolio had been a complete shitshow.

But her steely resolve during yesterday's exceptionally brief meeting impressed the hell out of me, especially when I tossed an empty portfolio on the desk and she didn't even flinch. Total power play, and she handled it like a complete professional. No excuses. No tears. Just simple one-word answers that told me everything I needed to know.

If she was as smart as I thought she was, she would eventually realize my bleak words of advice didn't mean shit. If interior design was her dream – her passion – then she would have to fight for it because I certainly wouldn't be the only one to bluntly recommend a different profession. Cat had talent, but she needed to realize that for herself.

"Motherfucker," I complained out loud, picking up the phone and calling the head of security. "Hey, Heath, can you do me a favor?"

Half an hour later, I calmly walked through the glass doors of Armstead Architecture with my head held high, projecting an ice cold demeanor. The happy hum dramatically shifted to frantic whispers and averted gazes. The sounds of a few pencils and rulers being dropped to the floor made me incredibly giddy inside.

Although Summer forced me to add more color to my wardrobe, I felt incredibly confident and powerful in my knee-length black pin-striped skirt and black fitted button down shirt tucked in. A thin black belt hugged my waist, and my black strappy heeled sandals added a few inches to my domineering height. My blonde hair was pulled back into a loose stylish knot with tendrils framing my face. I felt like a complete badass.

Christopher Armstead leaned against the door jamb to his floor-to-ceiling glass office and smirked at me. The arrogant bastard with thick blonde hair and matching facial scruff looked so damn sexy, and he knew it. His seductive blue eyes raked over my slim figure as his mind probably recalled our fun sexual tryst a few years ago.

Between finalizing his first divorce and meeting his second wife, he wasn't looking for anything serious. I had been more than happy to roll around between his insanely luxurious sheets for a few months before ending it to focus on expanding my business.

"Paige," he practically purred at me. "Welcome."

Heath from the security department brightened my day when he located the dumbass blonde through security footage and traced her steps to a male version of the dumbass blonde working at Armstead Architecture. Hello, David Greenlaw.

I rolled my eyes and stepped past him and into his office. "I need to speak with one of your stupid interns, Christopher."

Disappointment quickly flickered in his eyes, and I bit back a smile. "What happened?" he asked, closing the door to his office.

"One of your intern's familial relationships is deliberately fucking with my assistant, which means she's fucking with my business."

"Name the intern. I'll let him go immediately."

"David Greenlaw," I answered, with a frustrated sigh. "He's not a direct threat. His fucking sister is."

Stupid compassion. Why did the thought of Christopher firing one of his many lowly interns bother me? Especially when the little turd's mere presence managed to upset my staff. But apparently his psychopath of a sister believed he meant something to Cat, who worked like a true professional.

Even though her personal life mattered very little to me, it threatened her work performance. Maybe I should allow Christopher to fire the incompetent intern for unearthing my disgusting compassionate side.

"Can you even point him out?" I asked dryly, glancing out the lightly tinted glass wall and watching his staff anxiously shuffle blueprints around.

Christopher chuckled, leaning against the front of his mahogany desk and shoving his hands into the side pockets of his dark gray pants. "You of all people should know that I know everyone on my staff. However, they don't need to know that little secret."

My lips tugged into a small smirk as my eyes scanned the open work area filled with dozens of black-framed drafting tables and black-padded stools.

"The kid you want is looking at his phone," he pointed out. "Toward the back."

"Tell me about him," I said, narrowing my eyes on the tall muscular guy frowning.

"He doesn't say much, but he works hard. Doesn't seem to mind doing the dreaded coffee runs."

I turned slightly to find Christopher somewhat amused with his last sentence. My perfectly plucked eyebrows wrinkled with mild curiosity causing him to laugh and shake his head.

"Oh, Paige, I think you're losing your edge."

Scowling at his absurd insinuation, I flipped the middle finger at him as he continued to snicker.

"Did you not know your lovely assistant and my intern are a thing?" he asked mockingly.

"Never thought you cared about office gossip," I snapped, rolling my eyes and folding my arms across my chest.

Christopher's cute little revelation didn't surprise me at all. With her beautiful exotic looks, I figured she took pity on some poor schmuck to keep her warm at night.

"It's not gossip when it's true," he said smugly, pushing himself off the desk and standing behind me.

Oh, who the fuck cares? I thought dismissively, straightening my stance.

"Tell me, Paige," Christopher murmured softly. His minty breath gently caressed the shell of my ear, sending a small shiver down my spine. "should I let him go?"

The deliberate way he emphasized the last three words made me wonder for a nanosecond what the hell he meant. Just as I suspected his second marriage was falling apart, I realized I really didn't care. I didn't have time to play games. I had a fucking business to run.

"I really don't fucking care," I said sharply, heading toward the office door. "I just need five minutes. After that, he's all yours."

Christopher escorted me to a small all-glass conference room where the natural light shone brightly through the wide windows. The room was tucked away from the main floor, which meant no one could watch me yell at the poor schmuck or maybe make him cry.

Just as I glanced at a new message from Summer on my phone, the guy I spied earlier nervously entered the room. I bit down on my lower lip to keep myself from smiling as wild fear tore through his innocent eyes.

I'm going to have so much fun with you, I thought gleefully.

"Tell your sociopath of a sister to stay away from my staff, especially my assistant," I demanded, emphasizing the words "my assistant."

The kid's eyes widened in confusion and concern.

"Gail? What happened? What did she do? Did she hurt Cat?"

I ignored his questions and stepped closer, not even caring about his towering height. I had squared off against men twice his size and triumphed without a sweat.

"If I see her anywhere near any of my staff, I will personally make sure she's banned from the building."

"Yes, ma'am," David mumbled, shifting his eyes to the floor and digging one hand into a pocket.

Completely satisfied with my short and stern lecture, I turned to leave when the kid croaked out, "Ms. Ward?"

I purposely sighed loudly and glared at him. "What?"

"Cat's portfolio – I, um, I submitted it." He swallowed hard and took a tentative step back as if he expected me to lunge for his throat.

You little motherfucker! I thought furiously, wondering if I had the strength to strangle the naiveté from him. *This peon was seriously pissing me off. What was wrong with this fucking family?*

Cat's incomplete portfolio made sense to me now. I knew she was too intelligent to submit anything that ridiculous. I figured she was covering for someone, but I had absolutely no interest in investigating the matter. I just wanted to see results.

The guy had better be packing a damn baseball bat between his legs because I had no idea what my assistant found so appealing. Did she even know the devastatingly sexy idiot should have never even stepped inside her exclusive league?

Closing the small gap between us and practically crushing my phone in one hand, I snarled, "Do you know anything about interior design?"

He shook his head frantically. "I'm sorry," David said quickly and nervously. "I thought I was helping her – "

"Apologize to her," I seethed, not even attempting to keep my voice down. "I don't fucking want it. She took the blame because of your idiotic savior complex. Do you seriously believe she's incapable of doing her damn job?"

Christopher could fire his incompetent ass, and I wouldn't even bat a pretty little eyelash.

Running his trembling fingers through his dark blonde locks, the intern clearly looked distressed as his eyes glossed over. His love for Cat was obvious. If he truly cared for her, he would slap a restraining order on his psychotic sister.

Without another word or even waiting for a lame reply, I confidently marched out of the conference room and past Christopher's gawking employees with inquisitive eyes and open mouths.

I couldn't even stop my lips from stretching into a wide smile the moment I stepped onto the elevator. I totally nailed the compassion thing.

I felt so much better.

Coffee Makes Everything Better

DAVID

I was a fucking idiot. Seriously.

How the fuck did I end up sitting in my boss' office spilling everything about my relationships with Cat and Gail as if we were junior high girls at a sleepover? If he tossed me a bottle of nail polish and expected me to paint his nails, I would ask which hand he wanted completed first. One, he was still my boss and held the fate of my internship in his powerful hands. Two, I perfected the skill practicing on Cat while she read a book or played a game on her tablet over the past month.

As soon as Cat's badass boss practically skipped out of the office, according to Xander, I found myself fidgeting in a comfortable padded chair in front of my boss' desk. With his elbows propped on the wooden surface, the almighty and intimidating as hell Mr. Armstead stared blankly at me without blinking as he meticulously cracked his knuckles.

I gulped down my fear and panic when he finally spoke three little words, "Tell me everything." Where did I even begin? I had no idea.

"From the beginning, kid," he said firmly, answering the unspoken question in my mind, as he leaned back in his black leather chair.

I would have never in a billion years believed Gail's narcissistic nature could affect my career. Even before our parents split, she and I were never close but I was seriously a fucking idiot back then and thought she was the prettiest and nicest person. She was always surrounded by friends, giggling and smiling, and to me, she seemed happy.

And then I met Cat. I had promised my mom to give cross country a chance when my short and skinny ass wanted to try out for football with my friends. My mom rightfully worried about me being crushed among the sea of giants on the field.

I noticed Cat talking and laughing with her friends during practices, but she didn't catch my full attention until our first meet of the season. The handful of other seventh graders whose mothers deemed "football to be too dangerous for their babies" and I had been nervous as hell, waiting to run two miles in our first junior varsity race.

Two memories from my first-ever meet remained with me all these years later. The first being the pride I felt when the long-time head coach of the team patted me on the back and said my seventeenth-place finish was impressive for a first-time runner, especially in a race with about three hundred other kids.

However, I would have never landed in the top twenty if Cat hadn't screamed at me to "catch those guys" during the final stretch of the race. I was tired and sweaty and seriously believed I suffered from asthma with the way I had been huffing and puffing through the longest two miles of my life. I had been in no mood to catch a small cluster of three runners a few feet ahead of me. But when a pretty girl shouted my name and demanded I pass them, I felt an overwhelming need to impress her. Despite my skinny legs protesting the extra effort, I flew past the other guys and ran as fast as I could toward the finish line.

The memory of Cat yelling my name during the race never left my mind because that started my full blown infatuation with her. When I realized she cheered for every single team member at every race, I just admired and respected her even more for learning everyone's names. Because of her, I stuck to running even when my mom gave me permission to try out for the football team when I entered high school. A massive growth spurt over that summer had me a few inches shy of being six feet tall and added much needed muscle mass to my skinny ass.

I didn't expect my heart to hurt so damn much when Cat graduated from high school and headed to college in Iowa. Even though I hung onto every word whenever her younger sister, Liz, mentioned Cat's name, I reminded myself it was just a harmless crush and I had to keep moving forward. Especially when dozens of pretty girls flirted shamelessly with me during class and actually attended a few of my cross country meets to impress me. I was still a guy with two eyes and a libido.

I didn't regret staying in my hometown and attending a local college after high school graduation because I had no idea what I wanted to do. I had been content taking general classes, working at a local hardware store, and hanging out with the friends that stuck around the area during the first year at I stayed at home with my mom.

Cat never even crossed my mind when I decided to transfer to Iowa. My heart was still reeling from the amicable breakup with Annalise, and my mind was dealing with my mom's revelation Gail had slept with her new boyfriend. A new state, a new school, and new friends definitely kept me preoccupied until I accepted a summer internship with Armstead Architecture.

During a break on orientation day, I almost dropped my paper cup of coffee in the cafeteria when I spotted a familiar face smiling on the outdoor patio. I used every ounce of willpower I had to not bound through the door like a cute little puppy finding its forever home. Just watching her made me feel like the awkward and skinny seventh grader on the first day of cross country practice.

And Cat was fucking breathtaking as ever. And intelligent. And kind. And funny.

Just being around her over the next few weeks reminded me why I had a gigantic crush on her in the first place. I had every intention of asking her out, but something held me back. When I caught her eye-fucking me the day I needed help with stupid photocopier, my mind quickly formulated a plan to spend more time with her over the weekend. But then I opened my big fat mouth and mentioned my sister's name.

I knew my sister and Cat didn't get along for some reason, but I honestly didn't know the extent or even the specifics. Considering Cat was one of the nicest people I knew, I figured my sister did something to piss her off because Gail had a knack for getting underneath anyone's skin.

When Cat angrily threw out Marty Pullman's name, I immediately knew I was a fucking idiot. For believing everything my stupid sister said. For thinking she was actually a good person. For not having more faith in Cat.

The fire in her eyes. The fury in her voice. The tension in her entire body. All of it stripped away everything I thought I knew about Gail and revealed the hideous creature inside.

"Calm the fuck down, Marty," Gail had hissed, *yanking the kitchen cabinets in our mom's house wide open before slamming it shut with a loud bang. "Maybe if you didn't corner her between classes then maybe your balls wouldn't be so sore."*

Standing near the top of the staircase and hiding myself from her view, I had instinctively covered my junk with one hand as I wondered what the hell my sister was doing at the house. When I heard a muttering voice and movements in the kitchen, I had figured my mom somehow managed to leave work at the florist shop early.

Gail only dropped by if she knew Mom wouldn't be around and when she needed something, most likely alcohol and money. Hearing the name of one of the star basketball players stopped me from thundering down the stairs and giving my sister shit for stealing from our mom again.

"What the fuck did you expect?" Gail had snapped, irritation and impatience clear in her tone. "Did you think she'd fall to her knees and blow you in front of everyone?"

Even as an eighth-grader, I highly doubted high school was one big orgy where the popular jocks banged the cheerleaders or the cute nerd girls against the lockers during study hall. Thanks to one of my friends' parents not believing in safeguarding their kids' electronics, my friends and I had watched enough porn to know what was and what wasn't real.

"It was a fucking rumor I heard," my sister had practically shrieked. "I did fucking nothing. I told you what I had heard and that's it. You can't blame your stupid behavior on me."

Marty Pullman was the dumbest guy on the face of the planet, I had thought, not fully understanding why he had been mad at Gail for something he did. Awesome basketball player but definitely an idiot.

Gail had laughed maniacally as a deep thundering and furious male voice screaming obscenities traveled through the house. "Yeah, go ahead, Marty," she had taunted viciously. "You know I'll deny everything you say. Who will they believe? The senior basketball player who can't keep it in his pants for more than ten seconds or a sweet and shy sophomore who sticks to her circle of friends?"

Even then I had known my sister was definitely not sweet or why, but I also had no idea she was diabolical and devious.

A few days later the news about Marty being kicked off the team and being suspended hit my middle school. Various stories had mentioned him cheating in a class, getting caught using drugs, and touching a female student without her consent. Most of the kids easily believed he cheated, but I knew most of the truth.

But the moment Cat gritted out his name during her tirade, I realized she had been the victim and my sister had started the rumor. I even suspected Gail encouraged Marty to go after her, and the thought made me sick to my stomach. She was a complete monster, and I was a fucking idiot who defended her for most of my pitiful life.

And, of course, Gail denied every single word as she squeezed out fake tears and quiet sobs, but I already knew the truth. Even my aching heart knew everything she said and did had been a fucking lie to get what she wanted.

But somewhere between her superficial tears and my infuriating rants, I saw the truth. The way her mouth twitched upward a mere fraction and her dark blue eyes beamed with pride for less than a nanosecond when I mentioned the "accidental" haircut in art class.

I was a fucking idiot for even believing she had changed after sleeping with our mom's new boyfriend. Had I been that desperate for a normal sister-brother relationship? I had no reason to doubt Cat. The girl I had a crush on since seventh grade. The girl who smiled and waved to me in the school hallway. The girl who cheered for me.

I was so fucking lucky Cat had given me a second chance.

I would have even professed my undying love for her at the keg party if she told me to fuck off or if she walked away after my pledge to always choose her. I would have let her go with the knowledge that I loved her because she deserved to know and I had nothing to lose. And maybe the truth would have been enough to change her mind one day.

Even then I knew Cat was my endgame. She was the one.

Somewhere between noticing her on the cafeteria patio and kissing her on the empty sidewalk after playing darts, I fell in love with her. My mind wasn't interested in dissecting the feelings I had for her since seventh grade because my heart just knew. I just knew I wanted to spend the rest of my life with her.

While I loved Annalise and our simple relationship, she and I never talked about a future together even during her last year in college. We genuinely loved each other, but we both knew something was missing, especially toward the last few months leading toward the breakup.

The more time I spent with Cat, I realized my relationship with Annalise had lacked passion and drive. We had great times together, laughing over silly shit and talking about anything and everything, but we weren't passionate about each other.

Annalise made me smile and my heart race a bit faster. But with Cat, I seriously wondered if I had asthma because I occasionally found it difficult to breathe when I was around her. Anytime I caught a whiff of her light floral perfume or stared a little too long at her amazing legs, I had to discreetly adjust my boner.

I never believed I was a super touchy-feely kind of guy, but I couldn't seem to keep my hands off her. Not the overt grab ass or the obvious boob squeeze. I found myself high on the most simple and delicate touches. Holding her hand. Running my fingers through her hair. Placing my hand on the small of her back or around her waist. Resting my forehead against hers.

The night Annalise had asked for the truth about Gail, she noticed my bright smile any time I mentioned Cat. Annalise had been genuinely happy for me. While I had been surprised – even a little shocked – to discover how she had found her happiness, I was glad for her.

If I knew Cat wouldn't freak out, I would seriously propose the moment I found the perfect ring. Because our relationship was relatively new, I knew she wasn't quite ready to talk about a future together. I didn't plan to push her either because we had plenty of time. We were together – and ridiculously in love.

I was on a mission, however, to figure out her birthdate because I needed to buy my girl a California King bed. I loved spending time at her place because it was quiet and clean, but my poor long legs needed to stretch out and be free during the night.

Mr. Armstead threw his head back and laughed out loud while I furrowed my brows and secretly hoped he enjoyed the story he made me tell.

"Oh, to be young and dumb," he said, leaning forward in his chair, as he opened the middle desk drawer. "I'm not saying you're dumb, but the things kids do these days are pretty dumb."

I frowned, not knowing how to reply, as my boss searched the wide compartment among a pile of pens, notes, and business cards.

Should I ask him if my internship was safe? I wondered, slowly tapping my foot on the carpet.

I wasn't worried about missing the remaining paychecks, but a letter of recommendation from Mr. Christopher Armstead, architect extraordinaire, would look fucking amazing in my portfolio.

"Your internship is safe, kid," my boss said, holding a black business card in the air triumphantly. "Just warn your sister to stay away from the building because the next time she enters, she'll be leaving with cuffs around her wrists."

My eyes automatically went wide, and my palms started to sweat. The image of Gail leaving in handcuffs should she make another appearance didn't bother me, especially if she deserved it. But what the fuck did she do or say to Cat? Was my girl okay? I was two seconds away from whipping out my phone and calling her in front of my boss.

"Cameras are everywhere," he said, with a shrug, as he tossed the business card in my direction. "I saw the tape and spoke to Howard at the information desk. Your sister was clearly harassing your girlfriend."

"What happened?" I blurted out, wondering what the hell happened between Gail and Cat. "Is Cat okay?"

He shrugged again. "Nothing physical happened if that's what you're thinking."

A huge sigh of relief escaped my lungs as my boss nodded toward the small black paper on his desk. My eyes narrowed in confusion as I quickly read the name and information of a local mattress company.

"My brother owns it," Mr. Armstead explained, leaning back in his chair. "Tell him I sent you, and he'll give you a major discount on any bed you guys decide to buy."

What. The. Fuck? Was I being rewarded for my sister's bad behavior? What the fuck was I missing?

"I like you, David," my boss continued casually as if I should have already known this piece of information. "You seem like a good kid. According to Xander and Ben, you show some talent."

Thank you, I think? I thought silently, tucking the business card into the side pocket of my slacks.

"You were just caught in a really weird situation. And, to be honest, I'm not sure if I would have done anything differently."

"Thank you, sir," I said, swallowing my surprise.

"Take the rest of the day off and go talk to your sister, okay?"

"Yes, sir." I immediately shot out of the chair, shoving my hands into my pockets.

"See you tomorrow, kid."

Without a second thought, I hightailed it out of his office and wondered if I heard him chuckle as the door closed behind me. Taking several deep breaths to calm the building fury inside me, I headed toward Xander and Ben who undoubtedly needed to know every single word said between Paige's arrival and my exit from the boss' office.

I pulled out my phone and quickly dialed a number. As soon as a familiar voice answered, I swiped another deep breath to mask my anger.

"Did you talk to her, Annalise?" I asked bluntly, desperately hoping she knew my agitated tone had nothing to do with her. After listening to her tearful explanation for a few moments, I had one more question for her. "Where is she?"

A Bitter Taste

GAIL

ow the fuck did I not know? I thought to myself as I aimlessly paced inside my hotel room. *Trent and Annalise? Seriously?*

How the fuck did that even happen? My rage left little to no space for any other emotion like sadness or even pain. I had absolutely no desire to cry or wallow over losing my best friend and boyfriend in one day. The last time I cried over a boy was when Timothy Adlerman thought Angelique Ferris was "way prettier" than me in third grade. And the last time I genuinely cried was when my parents announced they were separating.

I had been ecstatic when Annalise called the other night and asked to meet in Iowa. I figured she and my dumbass brother finally realized they belonged together. I had planned to surprise Trent with the best sex of his life and crush Cat with some new intel from her younger sister, Elizabeth.

I had no good reason to hate Cat Coleman when we were in high school. I didn't exactly hate her, but I didn't like her. She hadn't been a loner or some strange girl back then; she was smart, friendly, and just average. Except I didn't love how perfect she looked as if she simply rolled out of bed with a fresh face and perfect hair.

Did I intentionally snip off a chunk of her long, thick dark hair because I hated mine so much and wanted her to feel miserable about hers too? Yes. Except the good little bitch looked fucking flawless and more mature with a layered bob the next day.

Preying on her insecurities and making her life miserable had been so incredibly easy and fun. Torturing anyone my friends and I didn't like back then was how we entertained ourselves, watching other people and relationships fall apart with our lies and manipulations.

The best part was cornering the teary-eyed losers and happily sharing our involvement. Poor Angelique Ferris tried in vain to blame me for her hilarious stripper performance at the school's talent show, but the stupid principal seriously had no reason to believe her. I wasn't even a member of the dance team nor friends with one of the captains that had a secret crush on my ex-boyfriend.

I had lost complete interest in him when I ditched his boring ass, but I saw an opportunity when the captain complained about Angelique bragging about the "magical first date" with my ex. Humiliate Angelique – more than likely ruining her newfound relationship – in exchange for a fake ID to rent hotel rooms and buy alcohol. The dance captain had an older brother who had been known to make the best fakes for a steep price to support his gambling addiction.

But now, I had every reason to hate Cat Coleman because she single-handedly destroyed my newly mended relationship with my brother. As I adamantly denied his accusations of bullying her, I mentally congratulated myself on a job well done. I had forgotten about pulling her skirt down during a social studies class, where fifty students noticed she wore plain white cotton underwear.

Never wear anything with an elastic waistband was an unwritten rule in high school. If I hadn't done it, someone else would have. Idiotic jocks like Marty Pullman always wore joggers that hung loose on their hips because they were more than happy to show off their packages.

But my own brother refused to believe me and cruelly advised me to never come back. The little fucker even changed his phone number so I couldn't even make a hollow gesture of calling and begging for forgiveness.

Cat deserved to have her self esteem shattered earlier today after seducing my brother with her wide eyes and sweet words. How could David not see she was a selfish and spoiled bitch? Even her parents and sisters knew the truth.

I rode on my high of devastating Cat when I met with Annalise, but a sense of dread quickly dropped into my stomach when I spotted my boyfriend with my best friend. Annalise immediately started blabbering and crying about not wanting to hurt me and trying to deny her attraction to Trent.

How the fuck did sweet and shy Annalise seduce my dangerously and sinfully sexy boyfriend? I just couldn't imagine the guy who loved fucking my pretty little mouth with his gigantic cock and pulling my hair during sex doing the same thing to my inexperienced best friend. I would bet good money my younger brother took her virginity and only fucked her in the missionary position.

Did I love Trent? No, but we looked so damn good together. I loved holding his hand or being by his side in public because I triumphantly savored the envious looks from women that clearly wanted to fuck my man. We were the picture of perfection.

With a commanding and confident presence and smooth hypnotizing voice, Trent held a promising career as a defense attorney as long as he didn't stay in Iowa. I badgered him to move to Minnesota so we could live together, but he refused and claimed he loved the area filled with cornfields and nothing else.

How the fuck did that even happen? That simple question kept repeating in my muddled mind.

Despite her denials, I thought Annalise still harbored feelings for David, never hesitating to ask about him whenever we talked. I didn't blink twice when I introduced her to Trent because the "bad boy" and the "girl next door" actually falling in love only happened in books and movies.

A soft knock sounded at the door, and I opened it without hesitation, thinking Annalise stopped by to beg for my forgiveness or Trent wanted to plead for a second chance. Seriously, what kind of man would choose a mousy, chubby brunette over a natural blonde with a fucking hot body?

Gulping my surprise as quickly as I could, I plastered on my game face as David glowered at me with so much rage I had never seen before.

How the hell did he even know I was in town? The only person who knew my hotel information was Annalise. Did she want David to check on me, wondering how I was handling her ultimate betrayal of friendship? But that didn't explain his obvious outrage toward me.

David shouldered his way inside the room without saying a single word and closed the door behind him. For once in my entire life, my younger brother scared the living shit out of me and I had no idea what to do.

"What the fuck is your problem?" he bellowed as I quickly turned my back to hide my shock at his furious volume and tone.

I plopped down on the couch, tucking my legs underneath. "Can't you see that I'm hurting?" I threw back at him as fake tears spilled down my face. "God, I'm such a fucking cliché. Dumped by my boyfriend for my own best friend."

David rolled his eyes as he paced around the open living room. "Knock it off, Gail. You never cared about either of them."

"That's not true!" I dramatically wiped the tears from my eyes and reached for a tissue I didn't need from the end table. "Annalise and I have been best friends for years."

"She was someone you easily manipulated over the years," he corrected, narrowing his eyes at me.

When did my idiot brother start seeing me for who I really am? I thought in disbelief as I clenched my jaw. *What. The. Fuck?*

David had been angry with me numerous times in the past but never like this. I knew which buttons to push to make him mad or forgive me because he had been so easy to exploit when he was younger. I was swimming in uncharted territory, especially when he ignored my calls for almost a year.

"You know she still loves you, right?" I lied, taking a wild stab in the dark. "Why else would she have called you the other night?"

My brother stopped pacing and ran a hand down his tired face. "She's pregnant," David revealed quietly. "She had called me for advice."

The air in my lungs suddenly crashed into the pit of my stomach. The extra pounds on Annalise's normal slender frame suddenly made sense. When Trent and Annalise admitted they were together, I quickly retreated with my head held high after throwing out a sharp, "Fuck you both." I had no intention of sticking around to listen to my former best friend repeatedly apologize as my ex-boyfriend stood protectively by her side.

But the unexpected pregnancy answered some of my questions. Jealous of my happy and perfect relationship with him, Annalise seduced Trent and figured he would step up and take care of the mother of his unborn child for the sake of appearances.

Oh, she's good, I thought, with a wicked smirk. I clearly underestimated my former best friend.

"What kind of advice did she want?" I demanded to know.

David sighed, sinking into a matching chair near the couch. "Annalise wanted to know who you really are."

"What the fuck does that mean?"

"That you're a puppet master, Gail, except some of us, like Mom, are smart enough to see that. You chose to live with Dad because he gave you anything you wanted."

He was right. I absolutely hated how I couldn't control our mom as easily as I could with our dad. He always shoved a credit card in my hand after I shed a few fake tears, breathed out heavy sobs, and threw out words like "broken" and "alone". Mom rolled her eyes and told me to "grow up" before she walked away from my fake blubbering.

"And Cat didn't need to even see you to know that you haven't changed at all," David continued, shaking his head, and smirked with amusement.

I rolled my eyes at the mention of her name and the lovestruck look on his dopey face. The wheels in my mind slowly rotated, searching for more ways to destroy Cat's life like she did with mine. My amazingly perfect life started to crumble the moment I recognized her having lunch with my brother.

Oh, she's good, I thought, pursing my lips together. Using my own brother against me was the ultimate payback for all the stupid little pranks I pulled on her in high school. Why didn't I realize her plan sooner?

"Stop," David said sharply, leaning forward and resting his elbows on his knees.

Noticing the flash of anger in his hard eyes, I asked innocently, "Stop what?"

"Stop thinking about whatever you're planning to do." His voice rose with impatience.

I gaped at him with complete surprise because he had never ever been able to read me before. From the smug smile on his face, he knew he caught me.

"Annalise isn't dumb either," David said, steepling his fingers together. "Even though she only heard your side of all your dramatic sob stories, she knew you were never a victim. Yeah, she knew you used her to get what you wanted, but you unknowingly pushed her outside her comfort zone and made her stronger. She remained friends with you all this time because she believed *you* needed someone."

I scoffed and shook my head. Sure, Annalise had been my best friend ever since our freshman year in college, but I had plenty of other friends that cared about me.

"She wanted to hear the other side of your stories," David continued. "And I told her what I believed to be was true."

"Which is what?" I snarled, wondering how my blood could boil and run cold at the same time.

"You seduced Mom's boyfriend because you wanted to hurt her for the all times she said no to you."

He wasn't wrong. Enticing our mom's almost serious boyfriend into bed took a little time and work on my part, but I knew the devastation in her eyes when she "caught" us would be worth it. Except her eyes darkened with disappointment and resignation. No tears. No screaming. No hysterics. Nothing. I had been delighted to ruin a significant part of her happy and perfect life, but I was also frustrated the impact wasn't as grand as I expected.

"Tell me I'm wrong," David said, running a hand through his hair.

I shrugged slightly, knowing he wouldn't believe anything I said anyway.

"Yeah, that's what I thought," he said sadly as he stood up and stretched out his legs. "Maybe you should think about growing up like the rest of us, Gail. And, maybe, you should think about someone other than yourself."

I snorted and rolled my eyes. He had always been a dreamer, believing in the good and easily trusting others. What a fucking moron. Cat would shatter his fragile and gullible heart the moment she became bored with him.

"Why are you even here?" I asked irritatingly, scowling at him.

"To say goodbye," David answered simply, heading toward the door. "I don't want to see you ever again. Also, stay away from my office. The next time you enter, you'll be leaving in handcuffs."

"Fuck off," I spat out as my temper began to rise. "It's a fucking public building. I can go in there whenever I fucking want. Talk to *whoever* I fucking want."

Before I could even blink, he angrily stalked over to the couch with a few long strides and towered over me. With his eyes blazing with rage and his body poised for battle, I actually fucking cowered in my seat.

"Not after the shit you pulled today, Gail," David gritted out vehemently, his hard eyes never leaving mine. "Do you think no one noticed your little stunt with Cat? Forget about the high-tech security cameras for a second. Do you even remember the older gentleman at the information desk? Or the barista in the coffee shop? Or even the fucking people that walked past you guys? Because all of them saw *you* harass Cat. You think Howard at the front desk won't hesitate to call security the next time he sees you?"

"She called me a twat!" I cried out weakly as my mind frantically tried to remember anything else besides degrading Cat.

"You go near her again, and I will fucking destroy you. You think you're the only one who can manipulate Dad? One word from me, and he will take everything away from you."

A sudden chill whipped through me as the weight of my brother's words sank into my increasingly desperate head. Ever since the divorce, David never asked our dad for anything and stupidly returned cash gifts and other stuff most guys would kill for. I seriously believed he was the dumbest motherfucker on the face of the planet when he turned down Dad's offer to buy a brand new car for his sixteenth birthday.

The fact he even mentioned involving our dad fucking terrified me. I relied on my dad's generous allowance and credit cards. Even though I barely graduated from college with a degree in English, I had no career goals or even a job. I did whatever the fuck I wanted whenever I wanted. My life had seriously been perfect until now.

"You're seriously choosing that bitch over your own sister? You're my brother!"

How the fuck did this day turn into my worst nightmare? I lost my boyfriend. I lost my best friend. And I've truly lost my little brother.

David chuckled without an ounce of humor and shook his head. "I'm really not your brother. You don't know anything about me."

Other than remembering he liked to doodle in sketchbooks and run, I didn't know much about him because I didn't care to know. Annalise – and fucking poor little Cat – probably knew more about him than I did.

"She will never be good enough for you," I fired back, crossing my arms over my chest, as my hands rubbed my arms for warmth. "Even her own parents don't love her."

My heart sank as his eyes showed no traces of adoration or compassion that a younger brother should have for an older sister. Instead I could actually feel his hatred and animosity through every fiber of his being.

"All the more reason why I love her," David said simply, with a wistful smile, as he took a step back.

"I need you," I choked out as genuine panic steadily rose inside my throat.

With one hand on the door knob, he gazed sadly at me. "You've never needed me."

"That's not true."

Without a second glance back or another word, David opened the door and left.

A loud anguished sob easily strangled the rest of my dignity as my body instinctively stretched out on the couch and genuine tears spilled out for the first time since I was thirteen. I was truly broken and alone.

CAT

"You are strong. You are beautiful," I murmured, sitting on the gray couch and lifting a bottle of wine to my lips. "You are enough."

After crying myself to sleep for a few hours, standing under scalding hot water in the shower, and eating chocolate fudge ice cream for lunch, I felt remarkably calm when I plopped my lazy body onto the couch and flipped the TV on to watch a marathon of *Law & Order*. Was it too late to study law?

I should be peeved at Paige for snatching my beautiful chocolate mint mocha earlier, but I was grateful she sent me home for being "sick". The time alone gave me a chance to sort through the never-ending questions plaguing my mind.

Did I have the right to blame my parents and my sisters for making me second guess myself anytime something good happened? Or was I so used to accepting the bad stuff that I didn't believe I deserved something good? When did filling myself with self doubt become a natural reflex?

Was it natural for a child to seek approval from the parents? And why didn't I write off my family sooner? No one – except for Mims – bothered to wish me a happy birthday ever since I moved to Iowa. Their well wishes during the holidays were forced and insincere in the presence of Mims because she didn't allow any of them to criticize me.

My grandmother was my rock. My champion. My defender. But even with her full and abundantly clear support and protection, my family still believed I was a spoiled and selfish skank. I should have shut them out sooner, but I desperately held onto a wisp of hope they would realize they had been wrong.

Maybe now was the time to be more selfish and less accommodating whenever they needed something from me. I had gotten this far without any of their support, and I would go even farther if I stopped secretly seeking their approval. Because, in reality, I never needed it in the first place.

With a soft sigh, I read through David's concerning messages, telling him I felt better and he should stop by my place after work. I had cried enough over the past few days so I was fairly confident I could talk without turning into a hot mess. Even though I believed crying wasn't a sign of weakness, I had never felt comfortable being vulnerable in front of other people.

David would no doubt see me at my worst one day. Even if he didn't have any comforting words, I suspected he would simply hold me and let me cry. He wasn't a complicated guy. He wore his heart on his sleeve and made me feel special and beautiful every single damn day. The guy actually enjoyed painting my toenails as I read a book or played one of my silly games on my tablet.

What scared the shit out of me was the simplicity of our relationship. With Gail temporarily out of the picture, being with David seemed incredibly easy and normal. I felt comfortable reminding him to put the toilet seat down and poking him in the side when he snored at night. He had no problem telling me I didn't need to buy more candles and nudging me in my sleep when I allegedly snored.

In previous relationships, my imagination and insecurities drove me to worry about stupid stuff like did the guy like me as much as I liked him or did he think about me when we weren't together. None of those silly thoughts even dared to enter my mind because David never gave me a single reason to spiral.

One adoring look with a small smile declared his heart belonged to me. One slow and tender kiss revealed how much he needed and wanted me. One protective touch showed he would do anything and everything for me.

Instead of worrying about the current state of our relationship, I caught glimpses into our future. Other than envisioning a devastatingly hot guy wearing the hell out of a suit and waiting for me at the end of a church aisle, I couldn't picture a life with any of my past boyfriends. But I saw something with David. Not the house with a white picket fence. Or the two or three children running around the back yard. Or the two dogs chasing after the kids.

I saw a life with him. One where we traveled. One where we stayed in on a Saturday night and binged watched Liam Neeson movies. One where we would argue about setting up a real Christmas tree versus an artificial one. And one where we would say "I love you" every day.

That was the life I wanted with David. Was I crazy to even think about a future after a month of dating and being ridiculously in love? If I didn't have the balls to suggest moving his gigantic bed to my place without being scared of running him off then I definitely couldn't ask about his thoughts on our future.

After taking another healthy swallow or two from the wine bottle in my hand, I heard a knock on the front door.

While my heart excitedly bounced inside my chest at the sight of David, I frowned deeply at the sadness in his eyes and the guilt written on his face. My stomach growled when my eyes spotted a takeout bag from my favorite Chinese restaurant in one of his hand.

If crab rangoons are in there, I'm definitely keeping him, I thought, biting back a smile, as he walked inside and headed straight toward the kitchen.

After placing the bag on the open counter space, David silently pulled me against his chest and wrapped his muscled arms around my shoulders. I slid my arms around his waist and buried my face in the crook of his neck.

Our bodies relaxed in the wordless embrace as his familiar and faint woodsy scent intoxicated me with so much happiness.

"How are you doing, baby?" he murmured as his hands cupped the back of my neck and a few fingers weaved through my hair.

"I've had better days," I admitted, the warmth of his touch and breath loosened the knots in my belly.

His fingers lightly tugged on a few strands of my hair, a simple signal for me to look at him. As soon as my head left the curve of his neck, his lips softly descended on mine. The soft, slow kiss eased my overactive mind and restlessness. A needy little noise slipped from my throat as my hands dug into the waistband of his gray dress pants. Feeling his tongue smoothly slide against mine, I pressed my body against his as desire blossomed inside me. David groaned lowly, his control becoming more possessive, as my stomach rumbled loudly in response.

I felt his lips curl into a smile before he reluctantly pulled back and chuckled.

"Somebody's hungry." His hands gripped my hips and effortlessly lifted me onto the counter. "Did you eat lunch?"

"I had chocolate fudge ice cream."

He rolled his eyes exasperatedly as he moved around my kitchen with ease and familiarity.

"Don't judge me," I said in a feigned warning tone as I opened the takeout bag and peeked inside. "Ice cream makes everything better."

I clapped happily after spotting the small paper bag filled with crab rangoons. As soon as I bit into the unhealthy appetizer, my eyes closed to savor the cream cheese filling and the crunch of the fried wanton.

"Do crab rangoons make everything better too?" David asked, with a smirk, as he held two forks and a bottle of beer in one hand and pulled out a backless stool with the other.

I nodded, popping the rest into my mouth, as one of my legs rested against his thigh.

"Ready to talk?" He dug his fork into an open container of sesame chicken. "Why didn't you tell me Gail stopped by sooner?"

I shrugged, picking up another fried appetizer. "I think I was more upset about Paige sending me home early and wondering if I could be fired for calling someone a twat."

"Whatever my sister said didn't bother you?"

"She mentioned you were using me to make your ex-girlfriend jealous and you guys were getting back together."

David quickly swallowed his bite as worry swept into his eyes. "You know she's lying – "

"Of course, I know she's lying," I interrupted, rolling my eyes and shaking my head. "Baby, I trust you. Your sister is a fucking dumbass for not knowing how amazing and kind her brother is."

He made a face in protest. "You mean tough and seriously sexy, right?"

"Mmmhmm." I smirked as I grabbed the second fork and speared a piece of sesame chicken from the open container in his hand.

"Wanna hear about my day?"

Wrinkling my eyebrows at the hint of secrecy in his tone, I tilted my head to study the slight amusement on his face.

"Someone special visited me at work too," David said smugly.

"Gail?" I frowned, wondering what she would've told him.

He shook his head. "Someone much scarier. Truly terrifying."

I twirled my index finger in a circular motion, encouraging him to continue, as I nabbed another piece of chicken and tossed it into my mouth.

"Paige."

The small bit of chicken that spent two point five seconds in my mouth soared through the air and landed near the refrigerator on the ivory linoleum floor. I reached for my wine bottle and chugged most of it as the remaining sauce strangled my throat.

"You okay?" David asked, setting the takeout container on the counter and lightly rubbing my back with his palm. "I suppose I could've waited until you swallowed."

I shot him a dirty look but smiled briefly before polishing off the rest of the wine. The fried goodies quickly dropped to the bottom of my stomach like lead weights as a million questions rushed into my mind. Paige took time from her hectic and highly important schedule to visit David? *What. The. Fuck?*

"Seriously?" I asked, studying his concerned face for any indication he was joking around. "What happened?"

"She basically called me a moron," he said with a slight shrug. "Called my sister a psychopath, and said you were the best thing that ever happened to her."

Rolling my eyes to the highest of heavens, I gave him my most disbelieving look.

"Fine," David huffed, with a small chuckle, as he stood between my legs. "She didn't say those exact words, but you do mean something to her."

I ducked my head and watched his hands lazily slide across my bare legs, leaving small goosebumps in their wake. The same hands that touched every inch of my body. The same hands that perfectly weaved through mine. The same hands that ran absentmindedly through my hair.

"Baby," he said softly, lifting my chin with his index finger. "If you didn't mean anything to her, she wouldn't have yelled at me. She had me on the verge of tears, Cat."

When his hand gently cupped my cheek, I leaned into it and closed my eyes. I honestly couldn't imagine Paige wasting her time and breath for me.

"She knows I sent your portfolio," David continued as I opened my eyes. "I am so sorry, baby. I should've had more faith in you when it came to your work. I want to see you succeed so badly, and I kinda thought you were standing in your own way."

He was right to an extent – I stood in my own way when I focused too much on my mistakes and failures. I wasn't learning from my errors; they distracted me from keeping an eye on the bigger picture. I needed to remember I would have other opportunities to show off my brilliance.

Because I was brilliant. *"You shouldn't even be in this field."* How many people told Paige the same thing when she first started out or when she created her own company? How many people were told to "go to hell" or "go fuck yourself" by Paige?

I was a fucking idiot! I wasn't about to tell my boss to go to hell, but I could prove her wrong. I survived a yearlong unpaid internship. I spent the last three months as her personal assistant and the unofficial office assistant. Despite her reputation of being a cold and badass boss, I wanted to work with her because her design work was impeccable and prestigious. I wanted to learn from the best. And I *was* going to learn from the fucking best.

"I imagine your boss knows what happened?" I asked, lacing my fingers through his.

David rolled his eyes and shook his head. "Yeah, after Paige left, he called me into his office and wanted to know everything. Like the full legit history."

"Did he fire you?"

He shook his head again, and I exhaled a relieved sigh. "My internship is done at the end of the month anyway. He gave me the rest of the day off to go yell at Gail."

"Wait? What?" My heart began to race as my mind frantically wondered if she knew where I lived. *Shit!* Checking the rearview mirror for followers didn't even cross my mind when I headed home. I would seriously suck as a professional spy. "She's still in town?"

"In a hotel room licking her wounds."

"Huh?"

David smirked as I knitted my eyebrows in confusion. "After Gail visited you, she met with Annalise."

"Okay," I replied slowly, wondering if his ex-girlfriend's secret played a vital part.

"Annalise is pregnant with Trent's kid."

"Wait? What?" My brain leisurely connected the dots to form a triangle. "Gail's best friend is pregnant with Gail's boyfriend's baby?"

"Yup."

"Is this what Annalise shared with you the other night?"

Squeezing my hand and nodding slightly, David said, "Yeah. She's not stupid and knew Gail manipulated people to get what she wanted. Annalise just didn't know the full extent."

Fuck. With her best friend and boyfriend gone, will she come after me again? I chewed on my lower lip with worry.

"Baby," he said gently, leaning his forehead against mine. "You don't need to worry about her. Paige practically banned her from the building, and I threatened her to stay away from you. If she goes near you, our dad will cut her off financially."

What? My eyes widened with bewilderment and skepticism at his promise.

"I don't get it," I admitted, fidgeting under his adoring gaze. "Why would your dad do that?"

"Because I would ask him to."

What? Why? David would actually ask his dad for a favor? For me? Slivers of self doubt slowly began to smother my little puffs of confidence.

"Baby," he repeated, clutching my hips and pulling me closer to the edge of the counter. "You and my mom are the two most important women in my life. And I will do anything to protect you from anyone."

I've never been important to anyone, I thought meekly as my heart pounded wildly and my mind attempted to process the truth bomb.

But I was important. Mims defended me against my family. Paige yelled at David for me. And David pretty much disowned his sister.

Cupping my face between his hands, he gazed into my curious eyes and carefully said, "Tú eres mi para siempre."

Holy fucking shit! The sweet spot between my legs clenched with an undeniable need at the foreign words as my mind screamed, *Marry this man right now, you hussy!*

"What did you say?" I asked breathlessly, digging my nails into his forearms, as my body melted against his.

I felt his lips tug into a smirk against my neck, where he planted soft panty-melting kisses.

"Guess you'll have to learn Spanish to find out," David teased, slipping his hands underneath my t-shirt and drifting his fingertips up and down my back.

A disgruntled noise escaped between my happy little sighs as his light touches lit a wildfire inside me. While I didn't have the balls to actually propose, I found enough courage to ask an equally important question.

"Hey," I said, brushing my lips over his, as my hands trailed down to squeeze his taut ass. "I think it's time I bought a new bed. Wanna test a few beds with me?"

From the immediate bright and wide grin and the sparkle in his beautiful green eyes, I knew everything I needed to know.

Delicate Daydream

COMING IN 2022

No epic love story ever starts with, "I fell in love with my best friend's boyfriend, and I'm unexpectedly pregnant with his baby."

Annalise Bowman understands her path to true love isn't a real-life fairy tale. She never expected to fall in love with her best friend's sinfully sexy boyfriend. And she definitely didn't expect to hear the words, "Congratulations, you're pregnant," during a routine doctor's appointment.

Ignoring her family's judgmental opinions and trusting her new boyfriend's promises, Annalise leaves her small hometown behind and moves into Trent's two-bedroom condo. Their mistake-filled beginning slowly straightens into domestic bliss as Annalise forms a tentative new friendship with someone unexpected.

But new discoveries, Trent's sudden busy schedule, and Annalise's controlling mother threaten to wreck the peace Annalise started to find with herself and her past. With her insecurities and doubts whispering in her ear, Annalise wonders if she even deserves a happily ever after.

Acknowledgments

Much thanks and love to my husband, Enrique, for supporting and encouraging me to write, especially when I decided to enter the 2020 Open Novella Contest on Wattpad at the last minute. He feeds the cats when I'm too wrapped up in my writing and helps me figure out the difference between "purposely" and "purposefully".

The word "thanks" barely covers my gratitude and love for Olivia M. Jones (*Someone Like You*) who took a huge chance on a freelance editor from Iowa. Our brainstorming sessions are the highlights of my day, giving my overactive imagination a creative outlet. And when I'm in need of a kidney, I will call in that favor and ask for yours. Then I would have a little piece of you with me forever. Um, that definitely didn't sound as creepy or stalkerish in my head.

How do I nominate Alyssa Evangeline for sainthood? Seriously. She searches high and low for "sexy" fonts. She continually nudges texts and images "two spaces" to the left – or right – at my request. She patiently and honestly answers my most frequently asked question, "Is this photo cute?" Alyssa takes my cover ideas and elevates them to a level I never knew existed.

Ivy Whitaker (*Home Sweet Hell*) is the queen of suspense, cliffhangers, and sarcasm, but her words of wisdom clear my mind when it overthinks and overanalyzes way too much. Even when she has a million and one things to do, she takes the time to answer my questions or calm my nerves.

Sadira Stone (*Christmas Rekindled*) and A.J. Skelly (*First Shift*) took time from their busy schedules to answer a stranger's pestering questions about self publishing and related topics. They welcomed me into the world of indie authors by sharing their journeys and offering insightful advice.

About the Author

Chessa Andersen smiles any time her friends call her "a genius," "brilliant," "an angel," and her all-time favorite, "a wizard." When she isn't arguing with her husband about being a wizard, she begrudgingly mows the huge lawn on hot summer days in Iowa and wishes she had trained her cats to use the toilet.

If she's not at her computer writing or editing, she's on the couch playing games or reading a book on her tablet. She wonders why she feels in-credibly smart solving expert-level Sudoku puzzles and if she would get into trouble by adding "NOT a USA Today Bestselling Author" above or under her name on her books.

Connect with her through Instagram at @chessaandersen. To catch her attention and make her smile, start the message with, "Hello, you amazing little wizard."